A Demon Called Grace

Danu's Secret Book 2

by Imogene Nix

LOVE BOOKS

SECRETS WORLD INTRODUCTION

As the Danu's Secrets is a continuation of the Blood Secrets & House Secrets trilogies, some readers may come into the series, unknowing of what has gone before. I've added the blurbs for all the Blood Secrets and House Secrets books to assist you to understand the world you are entering. I have also added the blurb for All that Glitters which is a crossover novella between the House Secrets and Danu's Secrets stories.

The Blood Bride Blurb:

Hope just wants to be an ordinary nestling. She went to college and escaped, but now she's back and there's a secret everyone is keeping from her.

Xavier is the new master of the nest, ready to welcome home the daughter of the house who he has never met. He's unprepared for the woman who steals his breath and enchants him.

Now Hope and Xavier must fight for lives and those of the innocents. After all, it is only by overcoming the rogues that they will have a chance of a timeless future together. But will it be in time?

Warning: If you love sexy alpha males that go bump in the

night, hot and heavy encounters and strong females, then this book is for you...

The Illuminated Witch Blurb

After years of struggling alone, Celina – a witchling of immense power – must find her place in the world of vampires.

Javed is building a new nest – the first new one in a century – and struggling to overcome his own demons, as an ancient evil stirs.

With Celina in danger, the demands of a fledgling nest and time running out, what are the chances their love can overcome every obstacle?

The Sorcerer's Touch Blurb:

Since the Slaughterhouse Rout, Daniel has nursed his abilities, but the decision he faces will change his life and those of everyone around him.

Whether the change is positive or not remains to be seen.

Cressida fears that history will repeat itself. Once before she lost everything she held dear, but after centuries of hiding she must face her past in order to

forge a new future. Has she waited too long and pushed Daniel away too well?

The darkness draws closer...

Just as the House Secrets book follow the original Blood Secrets series, so do the Danu's Secrets. However, below is a small taste of the House Secrets Trilogy (however Danu's Secret book 1, takes place after House Secrets Book 2.) As Dawn Breaks takes place at the same time as *Blood Secrets* "The Sorcerer's Touch," and is essentially a *continuation* of the Blood Secrets trilogy. To know how the Blood Secrets storyline ends, you do need to read The Sorcerer's Touch.

While the books *can* be read on its own, you have a better understanding of the world by reading the books which precede this one.

In As Dawn Breaks, we finally learn about David and his happy ending.

As Dawn Breaks Blurb:

Genevieve is many things, but no single title fits her quite as accurately as *'mutt'*—the one bestowed by her vicious ex-boyfriend. She's built a life, far from the family who've disowned her—one she's proud of—as a police officer with the Paranormal Liaison Division, and hiding from the world.
David is brittle from his experiences with his ex-wife Alexa, the truth his parents duped him his whole life, and he's trying to come to terms with the fallout of those beliefs, running a nest and feeling like an imposter.
A chance meeting between Genevieve and David opens up an opportunity for hope amid the grim realities of paranormal warfare. Trusting each other may be their only choice, but the past always bites back and this time is no different.

Edge of Night Blurb:

Pippa is terrified of her step father, Roger—a dangerous and cannibalistic paranormal. For years both Pippa and her twin Peter, have been prisoners, keeping his house and his home in order allowing him to pursue his desires. When Peter has a chance encounter with Simon, they finally have the support to make a run to freedom. Maxim is a fairy trying to put his life back together, rather than hiding as he's done for the last ten years. Niamh and Simon offer him a home, and a chance to finally achieve his desired career, but chance is a fickle thing, because next door is the timid Pippa and her twin Peter. She innocently ignites his protective side, against his will. Roger doesn't relinquish what is his easily, and the danger grows deeper. Pippa and Maxim along with Peter are moved to what should be a safer location, but the danger follows and while their attraction grows, so do the stakes.

House Secrets

How many secrets are hidden from view?

All That Glitters Blurb:

Genny and David had a wild and tumultuous romance, but now the were-pair must travel to Ireland where Genny will undertake her initial education as a leprechaun-were hybrid quickly.

As with all best intentions, things don't go as planned.

Padraic—Genny's father—is placing a wedge between them, and David is spectacularly unhappy with the growing distance between the pair. He just needs her back where she belongs... in his arms.

Genny doesn't see the danger at first, not until the night David doesn't come to her bed, then realisation hits, but with demons and secrets, demanding goddesses and lore all clashing, the two must work together as a couple.

They both know the only way to achieve that is with willpower and love.

The Downfall of Padraic O'Shaunessy Blurb:

Padraic is a leprechaun, long-lived and magical, but even those who have lived for millennia can still be surprised. Meeting Fenella throws him for a loop, because there's just something about her. Purchasing her family farm isn't just a whim for Padraic—it's the place where he came into the world with his supporters. It's imperative he protects the location of the portal between the hidden world of his past and the human world. Except there's these demons with other plans, particularly Marrer, and it's up to him to stop her. Fenella is alone and without anyone to help her. Her family is dead, and despite all the hard, backbreaking work she's put into the farm, she's lost it after generations held onto it. There's not much else to do but pack her belongings. That is, until the buyer arrives and asks her to stay.

What is this magic Padraic is claiming she has? Why are dangerous people threatening the property, and why is she so drawn to Padraic? Secrets abound as does danger, and the passion between them is fiery, only there's no certainty they'll survive it.

Danu's Secrets

Could Danu's secrets overcome the looming danger?

Please note:

The UK and USA share the English language, but there are many words that are spelled differently. Some words have extra letters in the British spelling, such as the word cancelled. In American English, it is spelled canceled. There also words that interchange the letters c or s and sometimes z. For example, in America, you spell offense and in Britain, it is written as offence. We also use the letter u in many words, such as colour and flavour.

These spellings are **not** incorrect.

This book is written in UK English to reflect my Australian/English background.

Ebook: 978-1-922369-72-7

Paperback: 978-1-922369-74-1

Editing by Pamela Tyler

Cover by Dexpress Covers

DEDICATION

Where to even begin? I feel like I somehow took a deep dive into a whole new world, one that I never expected to grow like this. When I wrote The Blood Bride (about thirteen years ago) I expected it to be a standalone. Naturally, that didn't happen like that. Ha! So, I wrote The Illuminated Witch and The Sorcerer's Touch sure that would be the end of the trilogy.

My daughter moaned and complained that she wanted David's story, so I relented and wrote As Dawn Breaks and that was swiftly followed by Immortal Consequences and yes there is one more planned (and as of writing this dedication, finished!) book for that series. But these characters made their own demands as Padraic O'Shaunessy reared his head, demanding his. That was it. But before I could write about his downfall, I needed to write All That Glitters... Notice a pattern yet? Uh huh. This was never my plan!

But for all that, I've enjoyed the world I've created. It's so similar to ours and has many of the same issues, and yet it's also just slightly different. Enough that the suspension of reality isn't so far removed from our lives.

Just in case you have a burning need to know, the last book in this world will release in October 2025.

Anyway, so as you can see I blame Charlotte all the way for the growth of this series... If you want to let her know, send me an email and I'll pass it along! Lol!

Ah yes, and while I'm on the subject of Charlotte, congratulations on your wedding baby girl, and welcome Nathan—officially—to our clan.

Thanks for reading and joining me on this wild ride.

Imogene
Feb 2023

CHAPTER

ONE

T he ocean was choppy, though Grace still found it lovely. It reminded her daily that she was still alive, in control of her own destiny, and though there were no easy answers for her, those thoughts were reassuring.

The letter on the seat beside her was also a reminder of realities, though not in such a positive manner.

Dear Grace,
We regret to inform you of the passing of your mother...

It wasn't unexpected, and neither was the fact that the notification had come by way of her parents' solicitors. Not after the decisions she'd made once she became an adult.

"Too much water under the bridge," she murmured, glancing at the envelope. The letter was three weeks old, having been sent to her mail redirection service and further sent on in a bulk mail bag to the ship.

Once she'd left her adopted parents' home, she'd made every attempt to hide herself from everyone who might seek her, including

I

them. She'd sold everything and taken a job aboard a small vessel sailing out of Brisbane for the Tahitian islands. All she had was a passport, bank account, and mail forwarding service. Her solicitors had been adamant they needed some form of contact. They'd claimed it likely some legal papers may need to be completed when preparing her restraining order on *them*—her adoptive parents. It was her solicitors who had suggested the forwarding service, and seeing as her expenses were few, it just made sense to keep paying for the assistance.

Had enough time passed that the one following her wouldn't come looking? She didn't know. She rubbed her brow, because while she loved her job and seeing the world, she did, one day, wish to set down roots.

"I don't know what to do," she muttered and flicked through the rest of the mail contained in the packet. She gasped, looking at another letter, this one from her own solicitors.

She didn't know whether to open it or not, because what else could there be? Hadn't she finished all the tasks she'd needed to complete?

A whistle blew, and she sighed, gathering up the parcel. "No time now." She rose, shoving them deep into the backpack she always kept beside her. The rest of the crew were streaming toward the deck which held the lifeboats. This was the least favourite of her regular rituals, but she knew that participation wasn't just mandatory, it could, potentially, save her life.

Luke sighed after another insanely frustrating call with the woman's solicitors.

"I'm sorry, Mr Jones, but Miss Cranston hasn't yet responded to our letter. And no, we can't give you any kind of estimate on the timeframe. We don't actually know where she is and are reliant on the mail redirection service to get contact to her."

What kind of solicitors didn't even know where their client was or how to get in contact with them? How did they make contact in an emergency? *Like now*, his brain added.

Not that Luke could even begin to explain why this was an emergency. After all, who would believe that a were would be hunting someone in such an unusual situation and her solicitors—the only listed contact—didn't know where she was.

Adding to not just the complexity, but strangeness, was that it was a case directed by a leprechaun from overseas via a third party, also from overseas. *If I said that out loud, people would think I'm nuts.* It wasn't that people didn't know weres and vampires existed, but when you got down to angels and demons things got a little hinky.

"Coffee for Luke! Luke!" the voice at the front of the coffee shop yelled, and he rose, taking the proffered coffee and bag containing a doughnut. The scent wafted in the air, and he inhaled deeply. True, the scent was interrupted by the ripeness of bodies jostling into the store, but he was a were, and his metabolism moved at a rapid rate, requiring constant fuelling. As for the scents? He'd grown used to them over the years.

He also didn't miss the appreciative gazes of the women he passed. Being a were meant he was well-built, with plenty of muscles in his arms, abdomen, and legs. His face was young-looking, and after all, he was only sixty-one. Courtesy of his Italian mother, he had dark, wavy hair. Nature had also been kind with a chiselled jaw, aquiline nose, and grey-blue eyes, and he'd made more than women fall for him over the years, simply by using the gifts he'd been granted during his adolescent years.

Time moved on though, and with that came focus. His pack had requested his assistance, and he was more than happy to provide it, especially when it came with a fat payment. "Which you'll only get if and when you track the woman down," he reminded himself.

He jogged to his office, three blocks away, and entered the building in the heart of Brisbane, answered the hail from the officer in charge of the entry. Ignoring the elevator, he headed to the hidden staircase, bolting up one, two, then three levels before pushing through the door and into his tiny office.

This back entry had more than once been a welcome relief from the rest of the company, and he liked it that way. His inner animal was comfortable with heights, but in his mind, the ability to come and go without being noticed was infinitely more important than a loftier office position. It also meant that if he needed to leave in a hurry, to satisfy the needs of his inner beast, he didn't need to run the gauntlet of the reception desk.

Settling into his seat, he swung up his legs, crossed them at the ankles, and gazed out onto what some called the 'river city.' The push to make it more modern had stripped from it the very features that set it apart. When he'd first come to Brisbane in his early twenties, there'd still been original colonial architecture, but the majority of that had long since been swallowed by the curse of modernity.

Luke grabbed the doughnut from the bag and took a bite, delighting in the warm, jammy squirt, the cinnamon and sugar dusting, and the still-fresh goodness. He savoured the flavours until the very last, licking the sugary residue from his fingers before turning to the milky cappuccino.

This time of the day was his favourite, because it was just him and food, but all too soon it would pass. So he enjoyed the break before rising and using the private bathroom—the only other demand he'd made in return for the lower office space—and washed up.

Files waited on his desk, an orderly pile for him to scrutinise, as he settled back in the seat. The first was the human resources recruitment folio. "I hate having to break in a new assistant," he growled, but in truth he needed one. Someone to handle the calls, which usually interrupted his work, arrange his meetings, and prepare his briefs for clients. They'd need to ensure it was someone who was open to his individual differences.

Within Freedmont, Jones, and McIntosh Investigations, he was an equal partner, and yet, unlike the other two—humans who'd been taken into his confidence years ago— there was a disconnect. They were aging and looked much older than him, and others bowed to their 'greater wisdom.' Yet at fifty and fifty-three they were both his junior. They'd all agreed, years ago, that the who and what of his identity was not to be discussed openly, at least not without his agreement, and they'd both agreed to the stipulation. So his secret remained intact, but Luke knew that soon he'd have to make some kind of announcement or move on.

He wasn't sure that was the outcome he desired however, as he'd built his life here, had built a home he enjoyed on a hundred and fifty acres just over an hour away, and he enjoyed his daily routine. The commute annoyed him, but he came and went at times that avoided the peak-hour rush, but perhaps it was time to open a second office, as they'd discussed nearly a decade earlier.

None of the applications in the folder appealed, and he scrawled a quick message on a sticky note explaining that he'd like to work with a recruitment agency, in case there was a better applicant.

The next folder was a complicated case, featuring not just one local character, but also his wife, the husband's girlfriend, and potentially three previously unknown children. "I hate these cases," he muttered, but he knew the wife had come to them because his reputation for confidentiality and willingness to keep digging until he had an answer were key to the success of the business.

He settled in to read the latest on the case, noting that the staff he'd assigned were making strides with getting to the bottom of it. Photos were enclosed of the children and potential mothers.

Until he had something more concrete, it wasn't an answer, but he suspected that this time, she might walk away from the husband. "Or maybe not. The last time the husband had an affair, she stayed." But then again, there hadn't been children involved.

THE KITCHEN WAS WINDING DOWN, and Grace surveyed the staff. Three others were smashed into the galley with her. The area felt too small for four, but they worked well together.

She'd worked her way up the ranks to take charge on this vessel, and the employees worked split shifts of six until eleven AM for half the staff, and nine to two for others. Then the entire galley staff were on from four until eleven PM to ensure food was fresh and the area spotless before they all retired for the evening. On top of that, she had ordering, menu planning, and of course, human resource tasks, and so on.

This trip they'd been at sea for six weeks, and she knew most of her staff were looking forward to the downtime that came with port calls, though she usually avoided them. For her, it was a time to catch up on sleep, go over menus, and focus on washing clothes.

As the captain wound his way into the galley, she got a pit in her stomach. "Grace, can I talk with you, please?"

Her fingers curled into fists at his query, and she nodded in the direction of the tiny cubby she used for her office. He slid the concertina door shut behind him, and the pit in her stomach became a yawning chasm.

"You're taking shore leave this time, Grace. I know you prefer to remain on ship, but you've been aboard for nearly nine months, and I've broken more than a few rules to allow this to happen. But that must change. Either that, or you're going to have to find another vessel."

Closing her eyes, Grace considered the options. Being at sea was safe. Very few knew exactly where she was, and even if they found out, they had to track the ship. She shook her head, trying to make sense of the mess she now found herself in.

"Grace?" The captain's voice felt far away in that moment, but she knew he was waiting for her to let him know. To give him an answer. The only thing was, there wasn't an easy one.

"When we reach Sydney, I promise—"

She opened her eyes to see his steady gaze, the set of his mouth.

"I can't allow that, Grace. I don't know what you're running from, but you can't hide on board like you usually do. The enforcement agencies are auditing all the ships entering the port, and I can't and won't put the ship at risk. Make a decision."

She had a good resume, could find work just about anywhere else, but it meant getting to know the routines and other sailors. But the captain was right. She bit her lip, considering all the facts. She could afford a few days while she scouted another vessel.

"I'm leaving the ship, Captain. Quitting. Once we dock…" She shrugged. Perhaps the time had come to move on anyway. After all, four years on one ship was a long time. Maybe the danger had passed?

His face creased. "If that's what you feel is best. You're a great cook, but a word from the wise?" He waited, eyes searching her face. "The sea is a mistress who refuses to take second place. Whatever sent you to sea, you need to settle it, otherwise that mistress will take more than just her pound of flesh."

Grace watched as he scanned the small office, the one she'd be packing probably later tonight, once the rest of the crew had found their bunks. She'd have to tell them in the morning of her decision and wondered what they'd make of it.

"We'll miss you, Grace. Your wages will be deposited into your account and any other entitlements, and I'll arrange for the paperwork to be sent to the usual location?"

"Thank you, Captain. If you'd be willing, a letter of recommendation would also be welcome." She fisted her hands once more, and he gave her a gnarly half-smile.

"It will be my pleasure. Fair winds, Grace."

He turned, opened the door, and stepped from the office, but he threw over his shoulder, "Don't take too long to decide what you want in life. Time and the seas wait for no one." Then he was gone, and she knew that her split-second decision had just changed her life.

Whether it was for the better remained to be seen.

CHAPTER

TWO

Luke snarled at the mess on the road ahead of him. The commute was shit! Three quarters of an hour to travel thirty kilometres, and of course, for the usual reasons. Breakdowns, crashes, and too many on roads clearly unable to cope with the growing needs of the city. How he wished the government would get their act together and really dedicate the funds needed to future-proof the roads.

"Mum wants to know when or if you're coming home. My mating ceremony is close, and you still haven't responded to the invitation. She's literally crawling the walls," his sister Paula growled. "We also need to know if you're going to use your room or not. If not, then we can put someone in there for the weekend."

He hissed, pinching the bridge of his nose. "I meant to get to that yesterday," he said.

"Well, clearly you didn't, little brother. Time's wasting away, and I need an answer. The caterer needs numbers, and I still need to finalise who's going to give me away, because I don't know if you're coming." Her voice was harsh with stress, and he cursed aloud.

"I'll be there, right? I said I would. And yes, I need my bedroom."

Being one of seven children, and the second oldest, came with a range of responsibilities. Their father had died nearly twenty years ago, and he'd had to shoulder the burden of pseudo-parenting. The twins, Alfie and Arlie, were little more than kits of three when their father died, and Alfie needed a male figure in his life to keep him from mischief, while Arlie needed a role model to show her that men were reliable and responsible. Caring, even.

Luke also knew that he just wasn't around as much as he should be. That too was something he needed to address. The other siblings were older and had more time with their father and those lessons in life had stuck. Alfie and Arlie were the only ones who still lived at home and hadn't yet matured, and their father had left when they were still infants.

"Then you need to let our mother know. She needs that card back this week, otherwise she said you'd be in for a world of hurt. Her words, not mine." Paula's voice wobbled a little, and Luke frowned. "Do it for me?" she asked. "I know you're busy, but marrying the alpha is a big deal. Everything has to be right or Nate loses face. That's not acceptable to me, Mother, or his family, Luke."

This wasn't anything Luke didn't know, but while Nate was a good man and an excellent alpha, he didn't live in the world of business. Didn't have control of a burgeoning multimillion-dollar business. Their pack was small, still re-establishing after it had fractured and broken after the death of Nate's father. This wedding between his sister and the alpha would be the first time most of the pack had come together. Luke knew the importance of the event. He wasn't going to let either the pack or his family down.

"Alright," he answered, hitting the steering wheel, and inhaling as, finally, the motorway started to open up while night settled in. "I'll fill out the card tonight and send it via courier in the morning when I get to work."

"Are you bringing a guest?" Paula's question was met with a frown.

"No, why?"

Her sigh echoed down the line. "Mother is getting impatient."

"I'm only sixty-one. I've years—"

"Not according to Mother. She told me to remind you Father was barely one hundred when he died."

"That was during the fracturing, Paula. Nothing to do with age, and more about his health." But the reminder that by his age he and his sister had both been born and looking to build their own lives was a reminder he wasn't ready to address.

"Alright, I need that card back, and you need to let us know when you're coming home. Mum wants to know what you're wearing, and you need to attend Nate's final power-circle meeting beforehand to deliver the details of my dowry. You also need to be on hand to witness the mate agreement documents."

"Sure. Send the dates to my phone and I'll have the receptionist input those into my calendar."

"Still no personal assistant?" He heard the frown in her voice.

"Not yet. But I'm meeting with four potentials tomorrow." He just hoped the recruitment company had listened, and these applicants did, in fact, meet his requirements.

"Alright then. I'll go, but if I don't have that card tomorrow afternoon—"

"I get it, Paula." His exit was looming. "I have to go. Love to Mum and Nate, yeah?"

"Love you too, lil' bro."

The line disconnected and he used the indicator to let the car behind him know he was exiting the motorway.

HEFTING HER LARGE PACK, while wearing the smaller one on her back, Grace left the boat. She didn't look back; regrets, she told herself, weren't something she could afford. *If only that rock in my belly agreed.*

What next? Biting her lip, she followed the direction the stream of crew had taken earlier in the day.

Her legs wobbled, and she put it down to not being on land for so long. She vaguely remembered that her gait had changed once she'd been onboard and guessed it would be the same for a day or two until she reacclimated to being on solid earth once more.

The air was humid, and sticky moisture pooled between her breasts and at the nape of her neck, and she tugged away her hair, needing relief. "It's only ten in the morning," she muttered.

Looking up, she noted the gathering clouds, heavy and grey. *Need to move*, she thought and hurried toward the chain-link fence which led to the parking zone. From there she could grab a taxi, and she hoped one was there, because for the first time in a long while, she regretted not having a phone.

At least this was a busy port, and toward the end of the dock there sat a cruise ship. Grace moved along, looking for a taxi, and on cue, one bowled up, disgorging its passengers with bags full of items, floppy hats, and lanyards swung around their necks.

Before the driver could leave, Grace rapped on his window. "Can you take me to Brisbane CBD?"

The driver nodded and popped the boot, allowing Grace to deposit the large bag, while the smaller one she kept close, and she clambered into the front passenger seat as nerves jumped and quivered.

"You been here before?" he asked Grace.

"I... A long time ago," she answered, wanting to avoid any direct questions about where she was from.

"You off the cruise ship?" the driver tried again.

"No," she said, hoping he'd take the hint.

They drove through the congestion, and the commute was worse than she remembered. Once he'd dropped her near the transit centre, she inhaled. Where to go now? The city had changed in the last few years she'd been travelling.

The information desk was teaming, but she spied a phone company booth and headed in that direction. She'd need a phone, and she looked at the options. There weren't a lot, and she was thankful, choosing a small one with limited options. It wasn't that she didn't know how to use them, but she didn't need anything more than phone, text, and the ability to get onto the internet. She paid for the service and handset, then on a whim asked the cashier, "Where's a good place to stay in town?"

The woman smiled. "There's plenty of hotels, but it depends on what you want."

"Privacy, quiet. A restaurant and…" She couldn't think of much else. She needed to find a bolt-hole until she could find another vessel. It probably would have made more sense to stay near the port, but then she'd still need to find transport, likely including a car. That would be harder without a place of residence, and she thought perhaps the forwarding service wasn't going to do the trick for that.

So the city seemed the best option. Besides, she needed to buy some new clothes, long-lasting and hard-wearing, given her jeans and t-shirts, not to mention her shoes, were really starting to show their age.

The woman suggested a hotel down near the botanic gardens. "It's where parliamentary visitors tend to stay. Not sure how easily you'll get a taxi, and it's a hike, but quite nice."

Grace hurried to find a taxi rank, and once in a vehicle she gave the name of the hotel to the driver. Thankfully, he wasn't chatty, and soon he deposited her at the door. While the hotel was older, maybe a building from the sixties or seventies, it looked well-cared for. The portico wasn't flashy, but inside the dark wood of the walls, the heavy furnishings were comfortable.

She booked a room overlooking the botanic gardens for a week, unsure how long she'd be staying, but it was better, Grace considered, to book for longer rather than try to re-arrange the stay after a few days. That kind of mess always made things difficult.

Even though it wasn't technically possible, the room was available early, so Grace was able to settle in, drop her bags, and consider her next step. Did she make contact with the mail redirection company, or should she check in with her solicitors? And how was she going to find another job? The job boards were all online, and while she had an email account, accessing it from the phone was the last thing she wanted to do.

"I wonder if there's an internet café around?" That would solve a big issue for her, she guessed, and if there were more than one, well, life would be simpler. She started hunting on her phone but only one appeared to fit the bill for what she needed. She had to face reality. She really needed to purchase some kind of device for accessing the internet.

Freshening up, Grace hurried about the room, dragging out the best pair of jeans and t-shirt she owned. All the rest were pretty thin and worn, and she honestly didn't think they were worth keeping. Sliding her boots over her worn socks, she sighed. She needed all new clothing.

Considering everything she owned was either stashed in the large backpack or stored securely in a rented storage unit—though there were only three boxes containing photos and mementos from her childhood—it was a sad way to think of her life.

"I'm not wallowing. I made choices, and I stand by them," she told herself. After all, it wasn't like there was much of value from her earlier years. Two years in foster care, then adoption to a couple who... "Not going there," she said, scooping up the room swipe and heading for the door.

The backpack on her shoulder swung around and one of the straps broke. "Damn it," she muttered. That was the first purchase she'd make. Her emergency backpack was far too important to leave to chance.

Luke's interviews went... poorly.

The first woman looked like a vagabond, with hair sticking up all over the place. The second stank of garlic, and while he liked that particular root vegetable, too much of a good thing was just that—

too much. The third was practically busting out of her top, and he could see issues in the office resulting from that.

He drank his water and sighed. This wasn't going at all the way he'd hoped, and if he'd seen the best of the candidates... he'd be severing bonds with the recruitment agency. The phone on his desk beeped, and he slid the glass to the tabletop and prepared himself.

"This one better be right," he muttered as he waited for the receptionist to show the applicant in. Checking the resume before him, it certainly appeared that she might fit the bill, but he'd wait and see. After all, hiring an assistant for an investigative firm wasn't just a case of 'she looks alright.' The applicant had to understand the complexities and subtleties of the task, needed to be discreet in all things, and have a passing knowledge of the law.

Three raps on the door, and Luke sat up in his chair, ready.

The door opened and in strode a woman who appeared to be in her late thirties. Her eyes were deep-set, hair tied up in a bun that could have been cast in concrete, the grey-white tones showing every perfectly groomed strand. "Thank you for seeing me today, Mr Jones."

He indicated the seat, and she settled, folder balanced in her lap. She was still. Perfectly so.

"Why are you looking for a new position, Miss... Phillips?"

She smiled, and for a moment, he fancied he saw razor-sharp teeth. Her eyes glinted. "Sometimes, when you're *different*," she purred the words, "you have to move on with regularity. It stops people noticing things that are inconvenient." Eliza Phillips slid a card across the table. "I was sent here by Nate Davison. I believe you know him well?"

Nate was Paula's fiancé. "And you know him, how?"

"He's cousin to my father's best friend. From childhood. I know what he is, and what you are. I understand more than may be apparent at first glance. I know you need an assistant who is comfortable with your needs. He felt I might suit." She shrugged and listed off her many varied experiences working in a legal firm, a hospital, and even with a government official. "The government official was concerned that there is growing chatter that I'm not aging, and he asked if I had recently had work done." She sighed and shook her head. "Cosmetic surgery. That's usually an indicator that my longevity at a place of employment is coming to an end. Especially when you're a were."

"Indeed," he responded. Her resume was impressive, and she appeared to know people in his world. The staff at his firm, or at least the senior members, were aware of his own nature. It would make choosing her an easy option. "And you live locally to here?" he asked.

She shook her head. "About an hour or so north of here. In a place called Narangba. But it's growing, and I'm not sure it will suit for much longer. I have three acres there."

He nodded, knowing it well, since he passed the turnoff to that neighbourhood daily.

"I need to make checks, but I have your number. If you're successful, how soon can you commence?"

"Monday would suit me. That gives me a few days to catch up on some family commitments, allow my inner creature to roam and…" She shrugged. "But if you need me sooner…?" The question hung in the air.

"No, Monday suits me fine." He stood and she followed his lead. "I'll be in touch."

He waited as she left, then lifted the receiver, pressed the button for an outer line, and dialled. He'd check her references, but for now, he had a feeling he'd found himself a personal assistant.

THREE HOURS LATER, Luke dialled her number. "Miss Phillips? Would you like to start on Monday in my office? We open at eight, so you'll need to be here at around ten to eight. I've quite a bit on, so you'll be hitting the ground running."

"Yes, I'll be there. What time do you close? I need to make parking arrangements, because the trains are... inconvenient, you understand."

He smiled, well aware of just how inconvenient they could be when you were an *other*. "We offer staff parking, particularly for those like myself with... divergent abilities. We close the doors at four, and you'll be here until about half past completing paperwork and preparing for the next day."

She thanked him again and hung up, and he tapped his fingers on the desk. He considered the situation. She lived north of the city and so did he. Was this the sign he was looking for? Was it time to get himself motivated to open that new office?

Rubbing his hands over his eyes, he slouched back in his seat, questions racing around in his head.

His phone trilled and he picked it up, the number known only to a few. "Hello?"

"It's me again," Paula's voice echoed. "Have you sent the card?" He dropped his arms at her question.

He cursed. "No, I'm about to do it now, but I've been interviewing—"

"Nate told me he'd sent a family friend in your direction," Paula interrupted.

"She's starting Monday."

"Well, that's good to hear. Nate wanted to employ her, but she would have cost the pack too much, and we're still trying to recoup after the expenses of the fracturing." Paula's voice was tinged with frustration. "If the others had been patient, we could have paid all the costs and come out in the black. All they needed to do was give us time to finalise the deals we had on the table."

Paula, like himself, had studied hard. They might be weres, but long before the coming out, as they now referred to it, younger members of packs had been encouraged to go out into the world, to gain qualifications and experience before returning with their knowledge and abilities to assist the greater pack. Paula had studied investment banking and had taken control of the financial well-being of the pack since she and Nate had got together, five years ago.

"Whatever happened to the agreement between the packs worldwide?" he asked.

Her sigh indicated that the answer to that question was complicated. "Only a few agreed. The Irish, Italians, Americans, and United Kingdom packs agreed with us. The deal fell through. It's why we couldn't access financial support we needed."

The fracturing had removed some of the architects of the pack's finances, along with a number of younger members who'd shown great promise in governance. They'd scrabbled afterward, filling the gaps as best they could, but the damage was done, and many years later, they were just starting to emerge stronger and more tightly bound than before.

"Right." Luke had little to do with the pack politics. He had enough intrigue on his plate daily without adding to it. His device screen flashed, indicating he had received a text. "I have to go, Paula. I've got the card here and I'm filling it out now and will get the receptionist to pop it into the courier system."

He hung up and clicked on the screen.

Your subject has been sighted in Brisbane, and you were right to be concerned.

We believe she's been working abroad for some time, though there is little to pinpoint her location. She's been the subject of a long-running hunt to try to discover her whereabouts. Those seeking her are unfriendlies, Luke. The group hunting isn't affiliated with either houses or packs either.

Today her bank account shows use at a hotel near the CBD, although it was a cash withdrawal, making it harder for us to pinpoint where she's staying, but if we've found that out, then so have they.

Maybe it's time to make contact with Padraic O'Shaunessy. He's got longer tentacles than we do.

"Not likely," Luke muttered. The little he knew of the man who'd employed him had only increased Luke's concern. He was clearly one of the 'other' but what... well, he honestly didn't know. All he could be sure of was some kind of affiliation to the American pack alpha, Simon. Luke had done his homework and reached out to the Lord of the Lycans before accepting this job.

The image attached to the message had Luke frowning. The woman was small, dark hair tied in a haphazard plait slung over her back. She carried a battered backpack, but it was the tension radiating from her that caught his attention.

He glanced again, noting that the building was downstairs from his office. "Damn!" He launched up, grabbing his bomber jacket to sling over his shoulders as he scooped up his keys and was through the door. He touch-dialled the reception then lifted the phone to his ear. "Kelly, there's a card on my desk. Express courier to my sister Paula. I'm likely out for the rest of the day."

He punched through the door to the stairs and took them two and three at a time, knowing that it was probably too late, but the urgency pounded through him.

Find her.

There was something more about the woman. Something that he didn't understand on a visceral level urging him to hurry. *To find. To protect.*

GRACE HAD JUST FINISHED at the computer café when she emerged into dull weather. The clouds hid the little bit of sunshine, and she sighed. "I hate rain," she muttered.

Her next task was to purchase clothing. Enough that she had the requisite ten days' worth. Less than that was unworkable on a ship, given she'd have to jockey for use of the laundry facilities.

She spied a small boutique, and while she didn't usually allow herself time to browse, the bright blouses caught her eyes. She stepped inside, fingers reaching for the pretty floral fabric. Roses had always been her favourite, especially those with the heady, spicy fragrance.

On a whim, she tugged the hanger from the rack and marched up to the desk without checking the price, just the size. "I'd like this," she announced, reaching for her purse.

"Of course." The woman smiled as Grace leafed through the cash and presented a hundred-dollar bill. "A bag?"

Grace shook her head. "It's fine. I'll pop it into my backpack."

The woman's face fell, and Grace knew what she was thinking, that the soft fabric would crush. It likely would, but she'd hang it in the bathroom at the hotel and steam it so the material would drop the creases and be right once more.

She stashed the item in her bag and was leaving the shop as she collided with a mountain. Or at least a mountain of a man.

"So sorry," he murmured and glanced up.

She caught sight of the grey-blue eyes which widened in surprise.

Deep inside her chest she felt something, like a click. As if a connection had been made.

Heat flared.

Panic set in. Body trembling and a wild fluttering in her chest warning her that she should do something. *Flee!*

Before she could move, hands grabbed her. Pulled her close. "Wait," the man said. "I've been looking for you."

She struggled against his hold. "Letmego, let me go, let me go."

"I'm not here to hurt you. I need to help you. I've been sent by the pack to—"

Her mind splintered. The pack. Weres.

Hunting for her.

Searching.

You'll never be free, a voice from the past whispered to her. *Never. You'll be hunted. Just like a dog.* She gulped, remembering what they'd done to the one they'd caught. *Blood. So much blood.* Grace almost gagged, even though it was only a memory.

Her fingers scrabbled, trying to release the hold, but the man was too strong. Terror shot through her, giving her strength and speed, just not enough.

"No," she muttered, squirming from side to side, looking for an escape.

He dragged her to the side. *"Stop fighting me."*

"No," she repeated, and this time she broke loose, moving with a burst of speed, heading for the exit. The doors opened, and she reached...

She'd nearly made it when he grabbed her. "Wait. They'll kill you if they find you. Let me help you."

Panting, needing oxygen in her starved lungs, while her body trembled, she stared at him. "You'll kill me." She was very aware of people gathering, phones in hand, likely videoing what was unfolding before them.

It was probably too late. All her caution and years of running came down to this.

CHAPTER

THREE

L uke could smell her terror. It poured from her body, sour and sharp, and he struggled to contain the instinct to hold tight. To shelter.

Why her? He couldn't explain the visceral reaction, only that it existed. The need to keep her safe was strange and dangerous by equal degrees, and he steered her toward the hidden doorway to the side. "Come this way," he urged, aware his voice was gruff and commanding.

She moved with him, her whole demeanour defeated. She slumped under his grip, and though he wanted to curse and demand, he just kept moving, inexorably.

Once the door closed, he sighed. "I'm not here to hurt you. I was sent by Padraic O'Shaunessy." He waited to see if there was any recognition, but she shook her head.

"I don't know him. Why would he...?"

It wasn't the time or the place to answer that question. "Come with me, and I'll explain everything."

He cursed inwardly as once more she shook her head and started inching away. "No. I don't trust you."

"Please," Luke answered. "If I was going to hurt you, I'd have done that the moment we came in here. I really do want to help you, Grace. I know who your father is, and he's the reason Padraic reached out."

Something flashed in her eyes. Was it fear? Was it hope?

"I don't have a father," she whispered.

Unable to help himself, a bubble of mirth rose in his chest. "You do. Everyone does. Now please, come with me." He reached for her hand. "I'll protect you." Luke pressed the elevator button before she could respond, and when it opened on a ding, he grabbed her hand and tugged her inside. "I'm a private investigator, and I was asked to find you."

She opened her mouth, eyes set on his, then closed her mouth again.

He knew she had questions, and he'd answer what he could, but the first step was to gain her trust enough to be able to contact Padraic. Then he'd wait and see what they wanted him to do.

There was also a sneaking suspicion that the danger was acute, because it cloaked her, and the taint of evil licked at the air around her, as if seeking her out.

"Who are you then?"

Her words surprised him, but the elevator stopped on his floor, and he waited for the doors to open, then tugged her toward his office, using his key to open the locked entry point.

"My name is Luke Jones. I'm a private investigator."

"That's not all, is it? You're... more." Her eyes glinted.

"Yes, that's true. But as to what I am—well, that's kind of personal, Grace. More to the point, why are you running?"

She cocked her head. "You don't know?"

He shrugged. "Your file is pretty sparce. You could tell me, if that would help."

She tugged on the length of hair hanging at her back, the plait now dishevelled from their altercation downstairs. "I'm nothing and no one. An orphan."

Her shrug was jerky, and he knew she hid something else. Something momentous... *What?*

Dragging out the file, he flipped it open so she could see. "This is all I have."

It wasn't quite everything, because the message he'd received wasn't in the folder, but he could get to that later. She flipped through it, fingers shaking. "Why does this Padraic O'Shaunessy want me?"

"I don't know. But we should find out."

THE WAY LUKE JONES watched her was discomforting to say the least. The terror that had poured out of Grace left her shaking as the adrenaline spike melted away. She slumped into the chair, the file before her giving nothing more away.

"So, you've been hiding, and quite well too," he said.

She nodded.

He sighed. Clearly, he'd wanted more information, but she didn't give away anything she didn't have to. Because, what if she had to run again? At least she had her backpack, and her hand caressed it. That was her safety net. Cash, and all her identity papers, along with the new phone were stashed inside it.

"How did you find me?"

He smiled. "I have friends who watch security cameras. They knew I was looking."

A flash of emotion speared her, and she rose, meaning to run. Because if he'd found her, so could others. That was dangerous.

"No one can get you here, Grace. You're safe."

Her hands balled into fists. "You don't understand. *No where is safe.*" The words emerged on a hiss.

"Not true. I've wards—the building, during its construction, was blessed and warded. Every girder and every wall contains enough holy water and amulets to keep the devil himself at bay."

She nearly answered *I got in*, but held that close. No one else needed to know anything about her.

"You can only enter if invited, whether human, demon, leprechaun, or vampire. I brought you in, so you're able to come and go. Trust me, I take care of those I protect."

"You bring people in, but what about others?"

Her question surprised him. He opened his mouth then closed it again. She'd scored a goal but regretted it too, because he'd obviously thought that the building was unbreachable. She'd just found a hole in his so-called armour.

"Let's get out of here," he muttered. He grabbed his jacket, the folder, and pressed a button on his phone when it beeped.

"Mr Jones? Is everything...?"

"It's fine, Kelly. As I indicated before, I'm out for the rest of the day," he growled then punched the button down, disconnecting so hard that the table rocked.

What was he? The thought lodged in Grace's mind but was shoved away as he grabbed her hand. "My car is in the private parking bay downstairs. Come with me. I have a totally secure location off-site."

He towed her out the door, and this time she didn't bother to fight. What was the point? Luke Jones was bigger and stronger than her.

He punched the button on the elevator again, and the doors closed.

She opened her mouth to speak, and he shook his head. "Not now. Wait until we get to the car."

The ride was quick, the elevator doors opening smoothly, and they stepped into the parking garage. It was tiny, with cars shoehorned in. His sporty vehicle was closest to the doors, and he pressed the button, the vehicle beeped, and he indicated she should be quick.

They'd just got in and shut the doors when two men came running toward them.

Luke swore and started the engine.

The men pulled pistols from their jackets.

"Fuck me!" Luke growled.

She shook in her seat. This was it; they'd found her and now she'd die...

"The car has bulletproof plating and the windows too," he said. "But it'll still leave a mark." He scowled.

She lifted a hand to her mouth, then bit it, hoping to ward off the hysterical mirth rising.

He pulled out slowly, as pings and flashes of light bounced off the doors.

"The tyres are specially spelled, anything to avoid them being punctured." He moved inexorably toward the exit.

"Why don't you run them over?" she asked, her voice shaking.

"Too much paperwork," he muttered. "And I'm not sure going to jail would assist."

She blinked then did it again as the men jumped aside and Luke gunned the engine as the roller doors blocking the exit rose.

No vehicles obscured the driveway, so he punched out into the street. The car gave a small screech as it hit the asphalt, then he zipped into the middle lane, and they were moving.

"I take it they were there for you?" Luke asked.

"Yeah, I guess so. Unless you've other clients who have people wanting to kill them?"

He laughed at her answer as she stared at him. "Not normally. Brisbane is pretty quiet like that. I've the odd cheating case, some fraud. Looking into high-level executives before recruitment. Fairly mundane stuff, you know? Missing people aren't my meat and potatoes."

She slumped against the leather seat. "This is a nice car, and you said bulletproof. How does a guy your age get to have a toy like this?" Maybe she could deflect the conversation?

"I'm not what I look, and I'm certainly not as old or young as I look either."

Confusion crowded her mind. "What does that mean?"

He turned and smiled, the car gliding to a stop as they waited for the change of lights. "Exactly what I said. Now then, we should ring this Padraic O'Shaunessy. Find out what he wants and why he has made your safety his number one priority."

"Wait!" There it was again, the flash of terror that chilled her to the bones. "What if he's in on who wants me? I mean... You saved me, right? What if he's the one behind all the attacks and attempts on my life?"

The lights changed, Luke drove forward, and silence filled the car.

Was he thinking? She hoped so. Maybe he was mulling over what she'd just said. Perhaps if she explained a little? Hope was something almost alien to her, but after the parking garage...

And what if that was a ruse? What if he's in on...

But why would he do that? He'd have to set it up, and going into that bloody boutique had been a matter of a split second. I didn't know, so how could he?

"I ran away from home at seventeen. Since then there have been several attempts to kill me. Poison, car accident, and there was even an attempt to kidnap me before I left 'home.' My 'mother,'" she said as she made air quotes, "told me I was being stupid. Why would anyone want me?"

The bubble of anger and hatred settled on her mind.

"I hated where I grew up, because they constantly reinforced that I was lucky I was given a home. I should have stayed in the orphanage. That I was useless." The words spewed forth. A lava flow that seemed to have no end as they scoured her.

"They adopted me when I was ten. I'd been in foster care for years. I'd entered with no memory, but I had injuries. Broken bones, cuts, and bruises. No one claimed me. No one knew me. It was like I'd been dropped into the world, and *no one gave a damn.* No one came looking for me."

Tears seared her cheeks, dribbling down, and she raised a hand to swipe at them.

"I have no memory of who and what I was before," she continued. "All I know is I had seven years of hatred, beatings, and
reminders I was nothing. Useless. A drain on the family."

She bit her lip hard enough to taste the tang of copper while the
organ in her chest squeezed ruthlessly.

LUKE DROVE IN SILENCE. Disbelief and a bubble of pure hatred rose in
his chest. *How could anyone treat a child like that?*

"Stop," he growled. "You're not useless or nothing. Padraic
O'Shaunessy—"

"I don't know who he is or why he wants me. All I do know is
when I ran, they came after me. One night, there was a fire. They
burnt down the hostel I hid in. They came after me again weeks later
and drove me off the road. I was shot at too. Someone wanted to end
me. All I had to go on was a message scrawled on a wall."

He glanced at her even as he drove. From the outside no one
would know the cataclysmic storm brewing in the vehicle.

"What did it say?"

"*I know you. I own you, and you'll pay. My people will find you.*" In
her voice there was a mixture of both resignation and futility. As if
she'd taken the words out again and again to examine them and
found nothing. He heard the rote precision of her recitation, and
from the corner of his eyes, saw that she shrugged and hunched in
on herself. He was sure she'd exhausted herself.

An urgency to protect and answer her questions forced him to
speak. "Then we find out who he is."

She laughed. "Yeah, good luck with that." Grace turned away,
closed her eyes, and he got the impression she was running on
empty.

CHAPTER

FOUR

Luke parked the car in the spacious garage and waited for the door to descend before reaching across.

The touch of his hand on her had an effect, just not quite the one he'd expected.

Grace's eyes flew open, fires licking in their depths, while her fingers curled, and claws emerged.

"Where am I?" Her voice had a guttural quality, and he cleared his throat, wondering what she was. *Clearly not human*, his brain added. But then, that wasn't a surprise, given the input of high-ranking *others* who were seeking assistance to find her.

"My home. I brought you here so we could talk. See if there's more I can do."

The nails retracted and her eyes took on the odd violet shade once more that he'd only dimly noted earlier today.

"I've spent years going over it, Mr Jones."

"Luke," he corrected her.

"Look, we aren't friends, and I'm not even sure why I'm here."

"Because it's safer than wherever you were staying." He spoke clearly, because he needed to take a moment.

She'd pushed back on using his name and that didn't sit well. He'd also considered the facts she'd told him on the drive, before she'd slept. The fury still licked at him. While he'd controlled it over the last hour, aware that she didn't need his emotional baggage adding to her situation, he also understood she needed support.

"Come on, let's get inside and I'll make you a drink. Tea, coffee, cola?"

She blinked at him. "Then what do you plan to do? I don't have clothes or anything else. Are you going to take me back to my hotel?"

"No. If I found you, then so can they. I've clothes here…" he said, and she tensed at his words. "My sister's clothes, which she left here. You can use them. Whatever you don't have, I'll get for you. Unless there's something you particularly need?"

Grace shook her head. "Not really," she replied and patted her hair. "I would like to clean up though."

Luke reached for his seatbelt and unfastened it, opened the car door, and stepped onto the concrete. "Come on," and he moved around the front of the car, skirting the wall.

She followed, though he knew it was unwillingly. He opened the doorway to the house, moved quickly through the body of the house, to the rear, where he—and she—could see the vista beyond.

Grace inhaled, and he turned with a smile on his face. Why it was important that she understood and welcomed the stillness, and beauty, he didn't know, but it was important. As a were, he was attuned to nature and those around him. So, if it was important on such an intrinsic level, he wouldn't ignore the urge.

"I love it here," he said simply. "The privacy and being close to nature were of the utmost priority."

"It's lovely." She stepped toward the sliding glass door and rested her hand against it. "It would be relaxing."

He opened the door and they moved onto the balcony. "Sit here and enjoy the serenity while I make some drinks."

He left her there, leaning toward the garden, and went inside to the kitchen and poured cold drinks for both of them, since she didn't make any choice. Luke welcomed the moment of quiet; it allowed him to consider the depth of his reaction to the woman.

Was it simply because he'd been looking for her that he felt a connection? Did that adequately explain why he'd nearly exploded, and the bubble he tried to ignore in his chest growing larger, almost suffocating him?

He clenched his glass, sweat beading his forehead.

Is it more?

Is this due to my nature as a were?

He shied away from that, not wanting to consider the ramifications. Paula's comments echoed in his mind. *Mother is getting impatient.* It couldn't be that, he told himself firmly, raising the glasses and heading outside.

"Here, this is for you," he said, and she jumped. He'd startled her.

Steering her in the direction of the outdoor table, he settled on a chair and waited for her to join him.

"Have you been here long?" she asked.

"About fifteen years," he answered.

"But you're only what, thirty-two? Thirty-three? You must be loaded to afford this."

He laughed. "I'm self-made," Luke assured her.

She frowned. "So, how old are you?"

"Would you believe me if I told you I'm in my sixties?"

She laughed. "Oh, that's funny. No, I wouldn't."

"My kind live long. We age slowly until our first century then not really at all, until old age."

Grace blinked. "What are you then? A werewolf?"

Luke didn't bother to control the growl that rose. "Would that bother you?"

Grace's eyes widened so that the violet of her eyes appeared to engulf her face. "No. Not really. I mean, I've never met one."

"And now you have," he muttered. "You've met a were."

"Oh."

As far as answers went, it wasn't much, but she at least didn't yell or jump up. Scream or run away. Some of the pressure in his chest released.

"I didn't know they were real. I saw the news reports when they... your kind came out to the world. I mean, I knew about the vampires, but since then, people have talked about all kinds of creatures, including angels and demons and dwarves and..." When Grace shrugged, Luke smiled.

"There are many kinds of *others*. Some are good, some not. Some neither. The only thing that has happened though is now that we're outed, our actions are more widely known. Scrutinised, I guess. It causes issues sometimes for the populace, because they attribute the actions of small groups against all *others*. For example, when Creedar was on the prowl, killing people—"

"I remember that," she interrupted. "He was killing vampires and making new ones. Attacking nests, including here in Australia. It was awful."

Luke nodded. "When Creedar was prowling, everyone thought vampires were dangerous. There were protests in the streets. When the weres emerged, they were blamed for attacks, labelled as freaks and murderers. It's taken years to overcome that stigma, and many of us haven't publicly announced what we are. Many still live in packs, and in Australia, we have several, because they splintered. Partly because the pressure before the emergence caused factions to form."

Grace frowned. "But why? I mean, there's an alpha, and they're what, elected by the pack, right?"

"Not exactly. Most alphas are born into the families of the existing alpha, which means bloodlines and strength are as important as love between alphas and their consorts."

"Who is your alpha?"

"Nate. He's a good man. Determined to ensure that the pack prospers."

"You know him well, Luke?"

He nodded and grinned. "My sister is marrying him in a couple of weeks. She's also the financial advisor for the pack, and since the fracturing—when the pack broke up—there's been a lot of effort gone into future-proofing." Luke wondered why he felt so comfortable telling her all this. Many were things that usually weren't shared outside the inner circle.

"You're uncomfortable, aren't you?" She narrowed her eyes and he sighed.

"I wouldn't normally share that much, Grace." He sipped on his drink, trying to clear his mind.

"Sometimes people do that. Tell me things they don't want to." Grace frowned. "And I don't know why that happens. It's just, I ask, and they tell me."

He waited but she said no more. They drank in silence until his phone trilled.

"Let me take this." He rose, moved to the end of the patio. "Hey, what's up?"

"We had an enquiry about half an hour ago. You were seen with a woman, downstairs." Jake Freedmont's voice echoed down the line. "Reception said you've left for the day. Is there anything we need to know?"

Luke frowned. "No. This is the private case I accepted."

"Ah," his business partner answered. "Then I'll let Gavin know. Let us know if you need any assistance."

Not for the first time, Luke thanked the stars for aligning and bringing the three of them together in a successful partnership. Gavin McIntosh was as reliable as Jake.

"If there's any further enquiries, let me know," Luke said, staring out into the backyard.

"Will do. Before you go, how did the interviews go? Have you found an assistant?"

"Yes. I've hired Eliza Phillips. She's also an *other* and should suit me well. I'm also going to look into the new office, north of Brisbane. It will allow us to grow and future-proof."

"Fine. Send through the proposal ahead of our next directors' meeting, so we can make changes to our future business planning based on the information."

They ended the call, and as Luke hung up, he glanced down, seeing the movement of a wallaby. He smiled because it was yet another matter of pride, that the regeneration of the landscape had brought with it the local fauna who'd been all but beaten back by progress.

Housing developments, encouraged by both council and the state government, were wreaking devastation on the land. Oh, they might claim that their interest in renewables and land management only extended to areas that didn't affect them personally. "Two-faced bastards," he muttered. At least here, Luke could make an honest difference to nature and the land he cared for.

He knew too that the pack was working hard to build sustainable agricultural enterprises. Paula and Nate had personally advocated to the elders of the pack the benefits of investing in these endeavours. And it was starting to pay off, along with their investments in grocery conglomerates.

While there was rising costs in feeding families, those who were regular customers of Discount Food Stores were the beneficiaries, and as Paula had recently explained, that meant a hefty number of new users of the service. Market gain meant increasing profits.

"Luke? What's wrong?"

Grace had crept up on him, and he turned toward her. "Nothing. Thinking about things that don't matter."

Her hair swung. "I don't think that's true. Was it about me? The phone call?"

There was no benefit in lying. "Yes. Someone came looking for you. One of my partners alerted me."

She started and he laid a hand on her shoulder. "You're safe here, Grace. You don't need to run."

"How can you be so sure?"

He smiled. "Trust me, nothing I don't want here can get in. Not unless I invite them, and I don't invite many to enter my sanctuary."

CHAPTER

FIVE

The bedroom Luke had allocated to Grace was comfortable. With a large bed, a flat-screen television on the wall, and a private bathroom. It rivalled her hotel room. Popping her backpack on one of the boudoir chairs, she moved to the window and looked out. The view was downright magnificent, and she walked to the bathroom.

Well-appointed with shower, tub, and toilet, there were choices of toiletries in hospitality-size containers. A toothbrush, still in its wrapper, filled the water glass along with a small tube of toothpaste. Mouthwash, cleanser, and moisturiser were laid out in a row beside a high-end handwash dispenser.

The towels on the rack were fluffy and pristine white, pairing with the grey and blue tinged room. It should have been too much, but the colours were pale and teamed with the gleaming white tiles to present a soft contrast.

She wandered back to the bedroom and opened the wardrobe doors, only to find jeans and t-shirts, button-down shirts, and maxi dresses, in a rainbow of colours. So much to leave behind!

As they'd entered the room, Luke smiled and said, "Use whatever you need. Paula has more at home and won't miss them."

"But they're hers." She couldn't possibly make use of another woman's clothing like that.

"Trust me, she's likely forgotten they're here. She's got more clothes than anyone would need in a lifetime, and it won't cause her to lose any sleep." He smiled and heat filled her insides at his smile.

She turned away and he'd left her then, to 'freshen up' and get comfortable.

Thinking on, Grace muttered, "Are they so rich that him giving away her clothes won't make any material difference?" That wasn't a reality she understood. Everything she had, she'd worked hard for.

The drawers contained underwear—she drew a line at second-hand there—along with shorts and nightwear.

On a sigh, she changed into the cooler shorts—amazed they fit—and a clean t-shirt. With hands and face washed she wandered back into the lounge room.

"Good, now that list?" Luke said.

She rattled it off, including the underwear and bras, not that he turned a hair, but she felt the heat of her blush. Luke sent off a text with her suggestions.

"If Paula can't do it, she'll get one of her staff. It'll be here before dinner, if I don't miss my guess."

"But... I'll pay, of course."

Luke simply rolled his eyes at her comment but kept silent as she looked around the lounge room. The room was tastefully furnished, with gold-coloured sofas, and cream cushions, the walls a pale eggshell colour, and blinds pulled back to reveal large glass windows. In the corner a pot-bellied stove reminded her that the winters could be cool, and she shivered in reaction.

"Okay," Luke said. "We need to talk. Sit down and tell me what you remember, and we'll see what needs doing."

Grace settled on the chair, unsure what to tell him. Was she prepared to give him everything, or was it wiser to only share what he needed to know? Biting her lip, she considered the man before her.

"Grace?"

"Hmm? Well, I was found by the side of the road, injured." She rattled off the date and saw his deep frown. "They thought there'd been an accident, but nothing was found. No car. No bodies." She shrugged.

Luke's frown deepened even more. "Nothing? Did they advertise?"

"I don't know," she answered. "I was in hospital for weeks, so... When I was released, it was into foster care. But I was unknown, with no name, and no parents. It was also around that time I needed... I had a psychologist and a neurologist, but they couldn't help me."

She remembered the turmoil and how she'd reacted.

"I wasn't easy, so I acted out," she said. "I was moved several times, while they tried to find out what I needed. In the end, there were no answers, so I was given a name. birth date, a birth certificate, and was made available for adoption. Only one family came forward."

"Where are they now?"

Her guts seized. "Dead. Both of them."

"Oh, I'm sorry for—"

"Don't be," she muttered. "They were awful. I don't even know how they got approved." The words were caustic and hung in the air between them.

"What... What happened?"

"What didn't?" was her answer. "They hated me, and I honestly don't know why they wanted to adopt me. I was treated like a second-class citizen from the day I entered their house. Second-hand clothing, only just enough food to stop questions. Holidays were the worst. I cleaned and cooked, and when it wasn't enough, they'd hit

me. Never anywhere others could see. The snide comments and..."
She inhaled, letting the frustration and fury at the memories of her
treatment wash off. She'd learned the coping technique as an adult.
A kind of 'I need to get through this' way of dealing with her
emotional reaction. "By the time they were finished, I was a mess."

"Didn't the psychologist or doctor—"

"They didn't believe I needed them, and the psychological care
ended as soon as they had custody of me. The few times I tried to ask
for help, outside the 'family,'" and again she used the air quotes to
ensure he understood her disdain, "it was put down to 'acting out' or
'denial of my situation' and I paid for that. Dearly."

A SHADOW of the pain of her past was easy to hear in her voice and see
in her physical reaction as she spoke. Her shoulders hunched, and
Luke couldn't begin to understand what she'd faced.

He closed his eyes, wishing he could remove her memories,
replace them with others that would make her smile. "I am sorry
that was your experience," he said and opened his eyes, letting her
see his reaction.

"I overcame it. But it was also around that time that messages
started to appear. On my windows on frosty mornings, cut-out
messages in the mailbox. It was like someone was watching me,
knew my comings and goings."

"But... Why?"

She shrugged. "I don't know. It got really creepy toward the end.
Things appeared in my bedroom while I was at school. Blood spots
on my pillow, or spattering the walls of my room. They said I did it
on purpose. That it proved I was some kind of unnatural creature."

"That... That's sick. I mean, who or what...?"

Grace shook her head. "I don't know who or why, just that things
started to get weird. The last month before I left, someone would go

into my room, drag my things from the drawers and dump them on the floor. The arguments got worse, and they…" Her breath hitched now. "They threatened that they would find someone to take me, someone who'd make me pay for the years of misery. I don't know if they had someone lined up to deal with me, but they would watch me, whisper things then stop when I entered the room. The atmosphere of the house changed too, like they were waiting for something, and I… I ran."

Everything Grace told Luke chilled him to the core. She'd been an innocent child, one who'd been dealt a bad hand. Then to be given to a couple who treated her so badly… He wanted to vomit, and the swell of nausea was difficult to overcome.

He stood, paced to the door and back, aware she was watching. How could anyone treat a child like that? In his mind, it was inconceivable.

She stood and headed out of the room, and he moved, grabbed her arm. "I'm sorry," he muttered.

"Yeah, that and cash gets you a coffee," she snarked.

He grunted and immediately realised that he'd done the wrong thing as her face twisted. "Don't grunt at me," she growled.

He shook his head. "No, I'm just trying to work it out in my head. But I don't get anything about why they'd act like that."

"Look, all this was a mistake," she said. "Take me back to the city and I'll…"

Luke grimaced. "No. Something about this situation is weird. You say they're dead, but the threats haven't stopped, nor has the danger. I wonder if you might have been thinking it was them behind the situation. Doesn't that strike you as odd? I mean, you turn up with no memory. You get bounced around then adopted by people who, from what you're telling me, didn't want you."

"Way to make a girl feel loved," she snarked.

He nodded. "I know, but let's forget the emotions for a moment, and I know that's hard, but just listen. They don't want you, but they keep you. The last months before you leave things get odd. Nothing about this feels coincidental."

Grace stared at him. "You think someone planned all this?" She blinked. "Why?"

"I don't know. All I can say with any certainty is someone was looking for you then. Did anything strange occur after you ran?" He'd found in life that even though people sought the easy answer, nothing in life was coincidental.

She nodded. "I found somewhere to stay, but the strange things kept occurring. Things would break, like windows. My car tyres were slashed four times in one month. I remember that because I stopped driving. I couldn't afford to replace the tyres, so I got the bus." She shivered. "Animals, like mice and rats, would be dead on the front step of the building..."

"That's all really odd, isn't it?"

She nodded again. "I didn't stay there for long, and I moved a couple more times and the things followed me. Like someone was watching. I... I bought an amulet after visiting a coven of witches. I had just got a job at sea, and I didn't want to be on a boat that sank or anything like that, so it was like an insurance policy, I guess." She laughed, but the sound was hysterical. "That sounds silly, right? 'Cause who would do something like that? Get an amulet?"

"That's not so silly. But do you have any idea what's following you? They've picked up the scent again, from what you've said."

She shook her head, and Luke felt frustration build inside him, the hardening of his chest warring with tension manifesting in tight muscles of his jaw. He worked it, trying to make head or tail of the situation.

"I know someone who might be able to unwind some of this," he said.

"Who?" she demanded.

"Someone. A friend," he clarified. "There's something going on, but I need to ask, and I'm not prying, but are you human?"

She laughed at that. "I guess, but how would I know?"

How indeed, he thought. He'd seen flashes in the short time since he'd found her, but she seemed like she had no clue. Maybe it was time to ring his friend. "Thea is... special, I guess. I'd like her to come and see if there's some kind of spell or hex or..."

Grace cocked her head. "You think someone is following me magically?"

It sounded far-fetched when she put it like that, but he needed to know, needed to be sure he could protect her while they got to the bottom of what was going on. No way was he going to call in anyone he didn't know until...

Why am I doing this?

He couldn't answer, only knew that there was some compulsion that forced him to ensure her safety. "Let me contact Thea. She may be able to make some kind of conclusions."

"Okay. But my things, at the hotel..."

He shook his head. "We'll worry about that later."

"I'd really like to have them. I... I don't have a lot, okay?"

Luke nodded. "For sure. But right now, here is the safest place for you, and no one knows where you are." He smiled and waved to the chairs they'd vacated. "Come sit back down and I'll call Thea. She lives close by, so I'm sure she can get here quickly."

They settled back into the chairs, and he dialled Thea who answered on the first ring.

"I was expecting your call, Luke."

"Well, that's good, and I suppose you know what I want too?" Over the years he'd got used to her divining his requests before he made them.

"Yes. When I was preparing my day, I had a vision. Anyway, I'll be there in a few minutes, I just need to grab the cake from the oven first." A ding echoed in the distance over the phone. "And there it is. Let me take it out and turn off the oven, then I'll be on my way."

He disconnected with a chuckle. "Thea's coming in a few minutes."

"Right. Okay then."

Glancing at Grace, he noted her sitting in the chair, pale, her hands gripped in her lap. "It'll be alright," he said, but in all honesty, it was only a hope right now, because he had no idea what kind of a mess they were in.

CHAPTER

SIX

G race was surprised when Thea arrived. She was tall and slender, with silvery-toned hair, her face lined with laughing memories lines which framed her mouth, and her eyes shone with pleasure as she hugged Luke. "It's been too long, Luca. You still owe me dinner from the last time I helped out with your investigations."

It took a lot to ignore the emotional reaction to the woman. It was hot in her gut, had her jaw clenching and fingers curling toward her palm. Grace took careful breaths to release the emotions surrounding her. It was strange, because after all, she had no reason for this reaction, did she?

He laughed and it shook Grace from her reverie. "True, *tesoro*. But I always make our time together unforgettable."

Thea laughed, voice tinkling. "True indeed. So, this is Grace?"

Muscles tightened in reaction. "You're Thea?"

The woman's smile died away. "Yes, I see your problem, except I can't help you beyond saying there is some kind of block. I feel it, and the aura is dark. A very dark grey." She turned to Luke. "You need help, because the colours of it are bleeding, darkening. There are flashes of red as well."

A buzz filled Grace's eyes, while the nerves starting at her hands began quivering and jumping before fanning out. "What's..." Her mouth dried, and she noted concern spreading over both their faces. Her vision wavered, and she gulped, because it was like the air in her lungs was being sucked out. She clawed at her neck. "I... Help me!"

Everything turned black.

LUKE CAUGHT Grace as she tumbled toward the ground. He'd watched as her eyes rolled back in her head, face paled, and her fingers clawed at her neck, leaving long, red scratches.

"Get her on the chair, Luca," Thea instructed, her voice steady, unlike his shaking hands.

He followed her instructions and knelt beside Grace, sliding a strand of hair from her face and studying the woman. In that moment, it reminded him that she was so alone. *Not anymore.*

Luke gulped and rose, facing Thea who watched him in silence.

"What happened just then, Thea?"

"It looks like a magical reaction." Thea stepped forward, sliding her hand through the air, and he knew she was reading what only she could see. "Whoever hexed her was powerful," she murmured. "Far more than I am. We need help." She glanced up at him, concern shining in her gaze. "We could call in Madame, but I think this is something even she would struggle with. Who exactly is she?"

He shook his head. "I can't tell you that. Her privacy is..." How the hell did he explain what he barely understood himself? "She's important to the case I'm working on," was all he said eventually.

Thea inspected his face, and he felt certain she read more into his answer than he was willing for her to see. "You're worried about her, and that confuses you." She nodded. "I can see several possible futures, Luke. Not all of them end well."

Luke grimaced. "I don't know what to do, Thea. I mean, there's something about her." He turned, running his hands through his hair. "I'm a fucking wolf, I don't do emotional deconstruction, and investigating my navel." The words spewed out of him, and he winced, because they also betrayed his emotional turmoil.

Her hand touched his shoulder, stilling him. "No, I know you're not a navel gazer. But you need to see clearly, make decisions from deep inside you. I can't guide you in this—it's not my role, and it would be wrong. You need to weigh the consequences and what's best for you. For both of you, without any coercion from anyone or anything else."

Luke turned to face her, not sure why, but it felt as if what she had to say carried a gravity he couldn't and shouldn't ignore.

"I will give you this piece of advice, friend. She's more than you expected but also very fragile. She's both strong and weak, dark and light." Thea's eyes misted over, warning him she was channelling a vision only she could see. "There is great danger, but also great reward. One cannot come without the other. You must surrender to win." Her eyes cleared and she swayed. "I can't see more, but I never can afterward." She sighed. "I need to go home, Luke." She turned toward the exit, and he followed her to the door, but he stilled her before she could open it.

"You'll be there if we need you?"

Her shoulders tensed. "If I can. Luke, I..." She shook her head. "I'll do what I can." She opened the door and left him standing there, confused and aggravated because her answer was as unclear as her vision.

A sound filled the air, like an animal in pain, and he whirled, running to the lounge.

Grace shook and shivered, moaning, and crying out. He bobbed down to crouch beside her. He laid a hand on her shoulder, and she jerked away, screaming, "No!"

He bared his teeth because there'd been so much fear in her word, her abject terror washing over him.

"Wake up, Grace. Please."

She shuddered, and slowly, her eyes opened. "Where am I?" she whispered and swiped at her brow. "What happened?"

"You collapsed. I caught you, but you've been out for five, maybe ten minutes."

Her mouth formed an 'o' then she sighed. "I remember. Thea, your friend. Where is she?" Grace struggled upright, looking around.

"She's gone. The only thing she knows is there's a hex. A very strong one that she doesn't think she can break."

"Ah," Grace replied, her lashes hiding her violet eyes. "I should leave then," she said, and she clearly meant it. For some odd reason, the idea that her very presence might endanger this—his home and his life—felt hideously wrong.

"No," Luke said with a shake of his head. "You need to stay here."

"It's too dangerous," Grace answered, attempting to push up, but he shoved her back against the chair.

"No. We'll work this out together."

Her laugh was cold. "I don't think so. I know what happens, I remember the times they tried to get to me. I can't ask that—"

"Good. You aren't asking, and I'm telling you. You stay here, and we'll work this out together."

"Why?" she asked, forcefully demanding an answer. "Why do you want to help me?"

"Because I..."

Grace sneered. "Because I'm some poor, helpless female? Because you're infallible? Because I'm a fool?" Her jeer stoked a fire inside him.

"No, because I feel..." He stopped, shoving his hands deep into his pants pockets. "Because—" The bubble of emotions in his chest almost choked him. How could he possibly explain?

"Because, because, because," she screamed at him, and it punched buttons he didn't know existed.

He reached out, gripping her shoulders. "Stop it, Grace."

"Don't tell me what to do, and let go of me, you... you, animal!" She threw the words, one of the worst insults for a wolf.

Something snapped inside him, fury and fire cascading and clashing. Each demanding ascendency.

He snarled and dragged her close, so that the hot wash of her breath bathed his face. "I won't, Grace. Because I don't want to." And he closed the distance between them, lips smashing against lips, and the kiss demanded her obedience. Demanded she accept that and more.

CHAPTER

SEVEN

Grace's fingers dug in, deep into Luke's collarbone, while he seared her, inside and out. She moaned, mouth opening just slightly but enough that his fire shoved itself in.

Need unfurled, a living and breathing entity that challenged her to take more. To fill the void deep inside her.

Tongues tangled and tussled, while lips ground hard.

Any kind of rational thought fled as they merged and joined, heat and light exploding behind her eyes, which closed during the sensual onslaught.

When Luke tugged away, she mewled, the loss of heat and connection... It was like ripping away a part of herself.

"Oh Gods," he whispered, his forehead resting against hers, his breathing loud and laboured.

Her hands fell away from his shoulders as the sense of hurt ricocheted through her. He regretted kissing her, so to protect herself, she tried to pull from his grasp.

"No, stay," he muttered.

Confusion filled her. He wanted her to stay but regretted… "What do you mean?"

He sighed, letting go of her waist but instead gripping her hands. "Look at me, Grace."

She didn't want to. Didn't want to see the remorse on his face. She glanced away, and he released a hand, reaching under her chin and making her look at him.

"I don't regret that, so much as I don't want to force you into anything you're unwilling for," he said. "Fuck it, not just that, but I want you to want whatever this is too."

She knew he saw the surprise on her face, as he grinned, a sort of lopsided smile that had her heart turning over. "I… You don't want me," she muttered.

Now he laughed, the sound full-bodied, and it made her body quiver in reaction. And not an unwelcome one either. "I'm not sure you could say that, Grace. You're a very sexy woman. A pocket of sensual heat, and a devastating kisser."

She gaped at him, her mouth open, surprise—and yes, a modicum of pleasure too—trickling through her at his words. "I…" Anything she said would sound wrong, so she closed her mouth.

His grin grew wider. "Now that we have that matter settled, I think we should settle on dinner. Paula is arranging one of her staffers to deliver the package, and they should be here soon." He helped her to stand, and she trailed into the kitchen behind him. "Do you cook?" he called.

When Grace laughed, Luke shot her a 'what's up' look. "I'm a cook onboard long-haul vessels. Not the slop a lot serve, but good food. I'm not quite cordon bleu trained, but I worked under a couple of very exacting chefs and worked my way up from general dogsbody to senior chef."

"Really?"

She nodded. "It took years, but I cook a mean steak, or if you want duck a' l'orange, I can manage that too. I'm rather keen on the

Julia Child version. Even Peking duck with the tiny pancakes is not beyond my capability."

Luke laughed. "Amazing. Well, I'm not going to ask you to cook anything out of the ordinary, but if you want to help me prepare some dinner, I'd welcome it."

"Anything in particular?"

He pulled a couple of thick steaks from the refrigerator—fresh, not frozen—and smiled. "Do these meet with your approval?"

She grinned. "Nicely marbled, firm flesh, plump with good fat distribution. They look perfect."

"Good. Have a look and see what you can come up with," he told her, and she opened the crisper drawers, finding limes, cabbage, sprouts, and onions.

"Do you have any chillies, peanut oil, and—"

"Check the cupboards, because I've got most things. Paula likes to cook when she stays here, and I like to cook as well," he clarified.

She found fish sauce, peanut oil, chillies, garlic, and ginger. "Nice," she said.

"Good. My brother, Oscar, has his own cattle. Angus Grey, so he lets us buy a beast a year. Weres eat a lot of meat, and we're pretty particular. I always feel sorry for those who buy from the grocery store. Thin, pale meat doesn't appeal to me or my inner animal."

She blinked. "No, I guess not. But how do you get on with urges..." Then she stilled and clapped her hands over her mouth in horror. "I'm sorry, that came out really rude." If there was a hole in the floor, she was sure she'd melt into it about now.

He sighed. "No, it's a fair question. Let me put it this way, I promise not to savage you in the night." His grin turned naughty. "Unless you want me to, of course." He waggled his brows.

She blushed. It wasn't like she was a virgin. Being on a ship, there'd been plenty of opportunities, but still... "Uh, I think I'll take a pass." *For now anyway.* She'd never been one to ignore the urges of her body, but with Luke, she was sure there was more, and that led to complications. *I don't do complications.*

She opened drawers, looking for utensils and bowls, giving herself time to think.

A knock echoed, and she breathed a sigh of relief as he left the room. It gave her time to concentrate on the task fully, as the sound of murmurs came from beyond. It was maybe ten minutes before he returned and, in that time, she re-centred herself.

"That was Paula's EA. She dropped off a couple of bags with the items you requested."

She blinked. "Oh, thank you. I'll fix her up—"

"No need. The client will settle any bills."

Grace tensed at Luke's answer. "I pay for my own things," she muttered.

"You can take it up with them later. For now, don't sweat it," Luke replied.

"Seriously," she muttered, aware he smiled at her outburst but didn't remonstrate with her. A moment or two passed and she rolled her shoulders, trying to release the pressure.

"Why did you go to sea? Did it appeal to you? Was there a particular draw?" He turned around and started to prepare the meal, buttering the pan, she noticed with real butter, not oil or margarine, and she felt a spurt of satisfaction.

"It felt safe. See, I think if someone is looking for you, they'll exhaust every option. But at sea is a whole different situation. They need to know which ship, then work out the vagaries of which port, and when." She stepped up beside him and grabbed the vegetables. "Asian salad?"

He nodded and Grace set to work, washing the vegetables, then drying them as she considered his question.

"I guess I was looking for a place to hide," she said, "somewhere difficult to reach, and on a boat seemed about as remote as you could get without heading into the desert. I don't like flies much, and I really love food."

Luke's laugh tickled something in her belly. "You'd have to love food and cooking to want to work in a galley."

Rolling her eyes, she sighed. "Not all onboard kitchens are pokey holes. Mine was large enough for four full-time staff. We took turns during the morning and day, but the night-time meal saw most of us on the clock together. Pastries and bread need to be fresh, vegetables and pasta, meats, and sauces. They all need to be made up ready for the crew, and they aren't overly keen on waiting until we get to it. Besides, they do a hard day's work, so they deserve to be treated well."

"Four, huh? Must have been a decent-size vessel then."

"It was a live trade ship. We carried veterinarians, the usual crew, and officers. These guys expect good food, and that's what we produced." It was a point of pride for Grace, and she watched him.

"It sounds like it's hard work. Did you enjoy it?"

Taking a moment, Grace considered the question. "Yes, I did. Creating the kind of food people want to eat is very satisfying. These guys—and the ships I worked on tended to be male crews and the odd other female in the kitchen—are used to good food. They work hard for more than the usual shift on land, and many don't get home for weeks on end. So, what we produce for them is nutritious, like they might eat at home, and gives them a sense of well-being."

"Your description of it makes it sound like you use food to counsel the crew." The steaks started to sizzle in the pan.

She sniffed because what he said was overwhelming. "Medium is my preferred level," she told him and turned back to the salad she was finishing.

"You felt like you belonged?"

She nodded. "Yes."

"Why did you leave your vessel then?"

Inhaling, she tried to find a way to explain her choices. It should be easy, but her emotions were caught up and formed a bubble in her throat. She cleared it. "I...I had been onboard for a long time. Months. The captain came to see me and said I had to take furlough." She tossed the salad, ensuring it was fully mixed before turning back to him in time to see him turn the steaks. "I didn't want to leave, but there was an audit on staff remaining onboard outside the allowable timeframes. I either had to take a furlough or leave and find another ship. I would have preferred to stay, but…" She shrugged. "I needed to do the right thing by the company and other crew."

"I see. Could you grab cutlery and plates? This is almost done."

She laid out the plates and started to serve the salad to the plates, and with a quick twist of his wrist, he turned off the burner and laid the steaks on the plates.

"We can eat outside, if you'd like," he offered, and she nodded before scooping up her plate and following him outside.

The sky was painted with reds and golds as dusk was settling.

"I love this time of the day," he said. "It's quiet. The birds have finished flying and are settling in. Small animals are returning to the burrows and holes, and the flying foxes haven't yet taken to the air."

"I don't think I've ever been somewhere so quiet at this time of the day," she muttered.

"Does it bother you?"

Once more Grace shrugged, not sure what she felt.

EIGHT

Luke waited, aware that the discussion had upset and maybe even frustrated Grace. He disliked needling her, not that he could explain why. Those emotions were best left unaddressed, he thought. However, he needed some answers before he could come up with a plan going forward.

Pouring a wine for both of them, he carried the glasses to the seat beside her. She'd relaxed, eyes half-closed as they glanced out onto the backyard.

"Here," he said, and handed her the glass.

"Thanks," she said, accepting it.

He noted she didn't sip immediately, but instead nursed the glass. Luke took a sip of his own dry chardonnay, waiting for her to be ready to talk.

A growl broke through the night, and her eyes widened and she sat up straight. "What's that?"

"It's a feral cat. There's a few out here, but they won't bother us. They can smell me, so they keep a pretty wide berth."

"Oh," she said and settled back in the seat. "I guess as an alpha hunter it makes sense you'd become an investigator. You must enjoy it." Her voice was low, and he strained to hear.

"Yes and no. The thrill of the chase doesn't always lead to a happy conclusion, Grace. Sometimes I find something that leaves me frustrated or angry or... There's even times I've discovered things too late to help."

"That must be hard for you. You've an air of power and competence about you. Finding things..."

"Once I had a task to find two girls. They'd been missing for over a year, and the police didn't have any leads. I found them in a shallow grave, but the thing was they'd only been dead a few days. I found the perpetrator too. Also dead. He'd detailed what he'd done, how he'd hurt them. Raped them. It was..." He cleared his throat, then took a sip of his drink. Remembering that particular case was painful.

"You felt powerless. Like it didn't matter what you did, it would never have been enough. That you'd let them and whoever set you the task down. You likely also felt guilt, horror, and devastation." She spoke quietly, and it shocked him that she could sum up his pain and sense of defeat so succinctly. No one else had understood.

"Yeah. I know now, it didn't matter, because while I was taking on the case, he'd been killing them. Right at the end, he understood what he'd done and couldn't live with it. He detailed it on video so whoever found them would know."

She reached over and touched his hand. "I'm sorry you had to feel that. Being powerless sucks."

"We need to talk about the hex."

Grace sighed, sipped her drink. "Yeah, about that. I didn't know about it, but it's not a surprise. I mean, yes, I had injuries, but none of them should have caused the amnesia. Doctors tried to break through until my adoption."

"We need help to get through it, but there's one other—"

A buzz sounded, and he swore, scooping up his phone and

reading the name illuminated on the screen. *Paula.* He'd have to answer it, otherwise there'd be no break from her nagging. "What's up?"

"A freak storm just came through, and the venue's been destroyed, Luke. What do we do?" She sniffled and he frowned.

His sister wasn't one to panic, but just a couple of weeks out from the wedding any contingencies she'd put in place probably were now unavailable. "What about the pack grounds?"

"What? No. I need somewhere green and open. Half the buildings are in need of renovation and—"

His brain spun… "What about here? I've got the meadow and—"

"Oh, Luke, you're a lifesaver. We can bring gazebos and tables and chairs. I'll need to pop around tomorrow, but thank you. I knew there was a reason you were my brother. I'll let Nate know it's sorted, and we'll contact all the guests tomorrow. I'll also get the caterer—"

"No. I'm not talking to your caterer or band or anyone else about power or where they can set up. You do that. We'll also need to figure out the parking, because they aren't tracking through my front yard," Luke growled, eyes closed in panic at the thought of dozens of people invading his privacy and tromping over the grass he slavishly seeded and nurtured.

"Sure. Nate and I will pop in tomorrow afternoon. Uh, did the bags get there? Is everything okay?"

"Yes, but I need to go now. I'll talk to you tomorrow, Paula."

"Love you, Luke," she said, and the call disconnected.

"You look like you've been hit by a truck," Grace said.

He placed his glass on the small coffee table and scrubbed his hands through his hair. "Paula's wedding is next Saturday, and the venue was destroyed in a freak storm today. She needs somewhere open, because she's… Well, let's just say, it was imperative to her and Nate. So, I offered the meadow at the back of the property."

Grace slid her drink onto the table, and he knew she meant to rise. "Oh, then I'm in your way. I can leave in the morning if you'd—"

Luke shook his head, reaching out with a hand. "No. You need to stay here. I just need to balance the investigation with family commitments."

"Luke, I... This is an important time, and you don't need me here in your way. Seriously, I can get a hotel."

CHAPTER

NINE

G race didn't know why she felt so comfortable here. It was odd. Lying in the bed with only the light of the moon to illuminate the room, there was a sense of peace and well-being.

She'd only ever found that on board a ship.

And as for Luke... Her body tightened just at the thought of him. The kiss they'd shared was downright explosive. Even now, the memory warmed areas that were reserved for pleasure.

Nipples budded and hunger roaring, she had options. She could pleasure herself; she'd done that a lot when the urge hit and no one suitable to scratch her itch was around. Or she could get up, grab a cold water, walk the deck until the need melted away.

The first felt wrong. Not her house, nor her bed.

The second was the only thing left.

She rose, aware that the light camisole top and flimsy shortie pants weren't much cover, but hey, what was the chance Luke would be prowling?

She moved quickly and quietly—years of practice drilled into her that silence was her friend—and headed down the hall to the

57

kitchen. The darkness enveloped her until she reached the room, flicked on the switch, and found a glass on the counter and the water cooler sat beside it. With a sigh, she poured the cool liquid.

The first sip wasn't enough, but she also needed more than that, she thought as she watched the sway of trees in the cooling air. Flicking the locking switch, Grace slid the door open and shivered a little as the cool air swept over exposed skin.

Stepping onto the planking, she moved toward the railing. In the distance, a creature loped along the grass. She sipped the water, watching its moves, mesmerised by its grace.

Once the glass was empty, she turned, slid it onto the table they'd eaten at, and glanced back at the sight.

The creature was gone, and she felt abandoned. "Well now, that's a stupid feeling, isn't it, Grace?"

"What's a stupid feeling?" Luke's voice surprised her, and she turned with a yelp.

Luke leaned against the metal frame, a pair of boxers the only clothing, so his body was surrounded by the light she'd left shining in the kitchen. The sight of him dried her mouth. Miles of bronzed skin, abdominal muscles hard and defined.

His legs were long and firm and covered in dark hair. And in between them she could see the outline of his cock, and she gulped because suddenly the heat inside her roared back to life.

"Grace? Like what you see?"

The words had her snapping her gaze back to his eyes. "I... Uh..."

Luke pushed away from the wall and stalked—yes, stalked—toward her, every move deliberate and slow. Drawing out the sensual moment so it felt like reverberations were beating through her nerves and blood.

When he stopped before her, she could barely breathe, and when she sucked in a lungful, it was heavy with the scent of him.

"I like what I see, Grace."

In the back of her brain, she knew he was giving her time, letting her pull away. She would be unable to claim she didn't want what he was about to offer.

Her fingers reached out, finding the heat of his flesh.

"Yes, touch me. Let me touch you."

Words had fled, and instead the void was filled by lust, and when he reached out, his fingers found the ribbon strap holding her top in place. His fingers toyed as he continued to watch her face.

"Please," she whispered, and his smile stole the last of her breath.

"I want to take this off you, slide it down so I can see your breasts. I wonder if your nipples are the same red as your lips? Will they be raspberry or ruby or strawberry pink?"

Her hand slid down his heated, silken flesh, toward the waistband that kept the material in place which covered him, and instinctively, she licked her lips.

He groaned. "You're killing me. I want you, Grace. I want to uncover your body, find your heat and sink deep. Will you let me?"

She nodded.

"The words, love. Give me your words."

Her strangled "yes" propelled him into action, his finger sliding beneath the strap with care, pushing it down over her shoulder as his other hand mirrored the action.

She sucked in oxygen, felt it catch in her throat as the material caught on her breasts, until he brushed the covering away.

"*Bella*," he whispered, cupping both globes, and his gaze darkened. "I want to taste them, slide my tongue over them and bite enough so that when I tug you cry out."

Her knees wobbled, as her insides melted. She gripped the edge of his boxers, holding tight, fingers trembling.

When he moved, hooking his arms beneath her legs, she cried out with surprise.

Several long strides brought them to the outside sofa, and he laid her down, devilry in his eyes. "Mine," he muttered, dropping down to pay homage to her body, mouth open before closing over one then the other distended nub.

She arched, reaching out once again, needing more. Needing him, hot and hard. lodged in her body.

Pulling on his boxers, she tugged until they dropped away, and he moved, hands sliding her panties down, so that they both were bare, the cool air ratcheting up the carnality of the moment.

His hands slid down her body, opening her, and his finger slid deep inside the moist cavern he found, and she cried out.

When Luke lifted his head, he panted. "I don't think I can wait," he muttered, and she groaned because neither could she.

Her eyes were half-closed as need demanded everything from her. "Please Luke, fill me," she muttered.

Now he moved between her legs, fitting himself then sliding with a single thrust deep within.

Heat and hunger demanded she move, so her hips lifted and gyrated, wanting every sensation, her fingers finding purchase in his shoulders, gripping and biting deep into flesh.

His mouth found hers, plundered, lips tangling while musk filled the air, surrounding them.

The tension inside her wound higher and tighter, and her legs wound around his waist, riding him as he filled her.

The edge loomed, and she let go, felt the rush of the orgasm overtaking her as he followed suit.

LUKE HELD Grace tight in his arms, wondering about the session of sex they'd just survived. Because he'd never engaged in anything like this, it wrecked his assurance that they'd pass the time together, engage in something that relieved their bodies, then say goodbye when the investigation was over.

His wolf growled its approval. It wanted more. It wanted...

He blinked. *I've found my mate.*

He couldn't claim not to know on an innate level that it was more than simply convenience.

A breeze slid over them, and Luke shivered. He knew they should close the door, but that would bring with it a conversation he was sure neither was ready for. Instead, he reached for the blanket Paula had left there and covered them both, because letting go of Grace right now wasn't an option. He held her in his arms and wondered what the hell he should do now.

TEN

Grace groaned and tried to raise her head, but it was wedged.

Opening her eyes, it took everything to not make a noise. She was naked. On the lounge under a blanket. Plastered against a hard male body.

She knew the hair and the scent. Luke.

He'd brought her here to keep her safe. She snorted silently, because safety had been the last thing either of them thought about last night.

The first rays of day were creeping above the horizon, and with great care, she tugged away and swung her legs to the side, preparing to rise.

"You don't have to go," Luke muttered, eyes opening.

She laughed. "I'm naked, in the air."

"You've never done that before?" He brushed off the blanket, rose, and walked toward her.

In the past, she'd always made her escape pretty much straight after, so the fact she'd slept with him as well as having sex made her wary. "I... No. I mean, on a ship..."

He nodded. "Yes, that would make it difficult. Too many men to ogle you. All that beautiful naked skin to drive them wild." His grin was huge.

It took every ounce of control not to roll her eyes. "I need to get dressed."

"Why?"

She gaped. "Someone might..."

Shaking his head, he stopped her from saying any more. "Nope. Not even Paula would intrude on me out the back."

Grace blinked. "Why?"

"Wolves are solitary usually, until they find a mate. Once they have a den, it's private. Sacred. If she's not invited to stay, it's considered—"

"Rude?" she queried.

"Yes, and more. Such an intrusion would be a cause for sanction. Paula likes rules too much, as do the wolf pack." He took Grace's hand and dragged her against him. "I know there's no agreements between us, but let me tell you, this morning you look stunning. Nature looks good on you."

He kissed her. It was soft and cautious, and it made something inside her unfurl.

"I... Coffee," she blurted out once he released her.

Confusion was a feeling she didn't like just as much as terror, and she shot inside the kitchen, needing a moment, more than a little aware she was still naked. Retrieving her clothes would mean parading in front of him. Besides which, she'd felt the rise of his morning erection. As much as engaging in sex again would be a plea-sure—and boy was it—she couldn't afford to get attached.

Her fingers fumbled the coffee as she heard him enter the kitchen.

He hovered behind her, and it took every ounce of her willpower not to turn and kiss him again.

"You're uncomfortable. I understand that, so I brought you

these," he said after she poured the water into the cups, and he held out her clothes.

She closed her eyes, even as she took the clothing. Thoughtful. *Urgh, I'm in so much trouble.*

"Thank you," she rasped and hurried to dress in the two very light pieces of clothing. "I... Would you get me the milk?"

She turned back and noted he too was dressed.

"Sure." He reached into the fridge. "Breakfast? I've bacon and eggs, or if you're worried about your weight, I have some of Paula's dry cardboard."

Grace quirked an eyebrow and watched as he blushed. "I didn't mean that as it came out," he muttered.

"Bacon and eggs are my favourite. I can cook that in a minute if you'd like?"

BREAKFAST WAS QUIET, and Luke wasn't sure how to open the discussion; a new problem for a man who'd spent years talking and extracting information.

"So, what is it you need to ask me, but haven't?" Grace enquired.

Could she read his mind? He blinked. "I need to know more about where you were found, if you've any abilities."

She cocked her head. "I never really asked much about where I was found, I guess because initially I was young and in hospital, then it wasn't really encouraged. I don't think they did either."

"So, when you started to get these messages, what happened?" He speared a thick hunk of meat.

Grace shrugged. "It was strange, because it was like someone was getting in and leaving them, but the person, or people, were invisible. I once said it was a ghost." She rubbed at her backside absently, and he understood the gesture immediately.

"They hit you for saying it was a ghost?"

Her mouth dropped open. "You can read minds?"

"No, you rubbed your backside, so I put two and two together. Did they beat you?" Fury coiled, like a reptilian creature, the emotion he detested was there, inside him. Dormant. It had never been like this before.

"I... Yeah. I learned quickly not to mention anything supernatural. No ghosts or weres, no vampires or... well, you know." She sipped her coffee.

"They were rabid Christians?" He tried to get a feeling of her childhood, but the bipolar way they acted confused him.

"Oh no. Nothing like that, but I think they were afraid that naming them would be like inviting them into the house. So it was completely forbidden. A lot of things set them off. Holidays were horrific. I spent more than one cleaning then in my room. They didn't believe in sparing the child or the extravagance of gifts or..." Her sigh filled the sudden silence. "I don't even know if they believed in anything apart from themselves. It was awkward. Other kids had parents take them away, make a fuss on birthdays, and had parties. I was invited a few times, but when I wasn't allowed to go, the invitations dried up."

"We need to get your records," he said suddenly. "Maybe there's something in there."

She stared at him. "You can do that? They told me I wasn't entitled, because they were official and that meant for the agencies only. I mean..." The confusion on her face was telling. Lies upon lies had been fed to her, and it was no wonder she'd fled rather than try to find out what she could about who she was.

"You can, and we'll get onto that this morning. It might shed some light on things." He didn't know if that was right, but it would give them a starting point.

It wasn't a lot to start with, but at least there was something.

Turning his mind to other things, he reached across, slid his hand over hers, thumb rubbing over the top. "I enjoyed last night."

She blushed a deep scarlet. "I... Thank you?"

"You're not used to the way weres think about intimacy, not having met one before."

When she shook his head he leaned back in his seat, releasing his grip on her. "Weres tend to be less buttoned-up. Sex for us is more like a gift. One we give and receive regularly. For many it's a way to relieve stress."

"You were stressed last night?" She raised an eyebrow, and once more he cursed the ham-handed way he was explaining their attitudes toward intimate encounters.

"No, but I'm trying to explain that for many it means no more than a good time."

Her eyes narrowed. "Do you see it that way?"

Unstable ground here. "No, not exactly. I believe in mates and predestination. I know one day my mate will make herself known. The connection we'll share will be unlike anything else. It was like that for my parents, and for Paula and Nate."

"So, you were what, checking to see if it was me?" She laughed, as if disbelieving what he'd already learned. *Don't tell her. She's not ready.*

"I just want you to know that I respect you. Anything we choose to do will be consensual."

"Oh, okay." She rose, grabbing the plates, clearly uncomfortable.

"Grace?" She blushed but looked at him. "I'd like to continue this liaison."

Her single nod wasn't really an agreement, but neither was it a request to not continue. He would have preferred her to make some kind of determination, but she needed time. She'd never really been able to be in charge of her own destiny, and he wasn't going to strip this opportunity from her. No matter that it also affected him.

His phone buzzed, and looking down, he saw a text from Paula.

I'll be there in a few minutes. Nate is following, and the caterer and planner are with me. Can we meet you at the house? There are releases that need signing.

It didn't really suit him, but he looked up at Grace who'd

retreated to the kitchen. "You should leave that for now," he called out. "Paula will be here in a few, and she's bringing a crowd."

Grace paled and he rose.

She shook her head. "I'll go dress and make myself scarce then."

He paced toward her. "No, you'll get dressed, then I'd really like you to meet my sister." He lifted his hands to her shoulders, resting them there to accentuate what he needed to tell her.

Her mouth fell open. "You want me to meet her? But, why?"

"Because I think you'd like her, and I think she'll like you too. You don't need to hide away. I'm not your adoptive parents, Grace. While you're staying here, you're a valued member of the household."

"Oh," she said. "Then I better go find some clothes." She moved and he withdrew his hands, and she slipped away. He watched as she left the room.

Looking down, he realised he was still in boxers, so he hurried to his own room, grabbing clothes to throw on—a wrinkled shirt and jeans—then shoved his feet into a pair of slides. Sprinting to his bathroom, he brushed his teeth, and not a moment too soon as a knock echoed through the house.

He rushed to the door and swung it open. Paula smiled at him, and he ushered them all in.

"Well now, here's my favourite brother," Paula said with a grin.

"The one who's letting you and all your guests invade my private space for your wedding, so of course I'm your favourite."

She launched onto her toes and kissed his cheek. "This is Sienna, the caterer, and Francis, who's in charge of putting everything together. He's got papers for you to sign."

Luke held out his hand and Francis, an older man with pale blue eyes, extended a folder. "It's quite the house you have here. But your protective wards will make it difficult for the guests," he added.

"The back meadow is free of wards. I had that left open as a neutral ground for weres to meet." Luke didn't feel inclined to tell him that he didn't want people at his house; after all, that might sound churlish.

"Luke is very private. We respect his privacy, and it was very kind of him to allow us to have the wedding there. It's perfect. You'll see what I mean when we go down there," Paula explained as Luke saw Grace step into the hall. Paula's eyes widened. "Oh, you have a guest... Of course, that's why Ella delivered her packages."

Grace hovered by the door, but Luke called her over. "Come meet my sister, Grace."

She moved slowly, as if unwilling, and he understood, based on what she'd told him of her childhood. It wasn't that she didn't want to meet his sister, but she was wary.

Strange I already can read her emotional state. Perhaps it was something to do with understanding his mate.

CHAPTER

ELEVEN

Hovering near the door wasn't an option when Luke called her over, Grace thought. So she walked slowly toward the group, feeling as if any second someone would tell her to get lost. That it was none of her business.

Instead, the woman in charge—and Grace could tell that because she spoke quickly and appeared very comfortable—smiled at her. "I'm Paula, and you must be Grace! I do recall now my brother mentioning you and asking my assistant Ella to pick up some basics."

The welcome *felt* genuine.

"Hi," Grace muttered.

Luke reached out and pulled Grace close, and she noted that Paula didn't miss the proprietary way he slid his arm around her waist, anchoring her against him.

"So, Luca. If you'll sign these papers, we can go down to the meadow. Of course, you'll need to come with us. I want to be sure you're comfortable with the placement of parking and the gazebo for the feast." Paula's words tumbled out in a rush.

"Yeah, okay, let me get a look at those papers. And don't call me

Luca. I'm Luke. An adult." He said the words absently, by rote, but with a half-smile. He released Grace long enough to flip through the cardboard folder he held, scanned whatever they contained, then took the pen the man offered and scrawled his signature. "Here," he said and handed the folder back.

"Excellent," the man said. "I'll arrange for these to be entered into our system, and we'll scan and send you an email of them later today." Even though he spoke quietly, Grace had the impression the man was looking at her.

Her skin itched, and she wondered if it was a reaction to something on the clothes or in the body wash she'd used in the shower last night.

The unnamed man stepped closer, sniffed the air, and frowned. "What is that smell?"

Luke turned and so did Paula, and Grace frowned. The other woman standing there also frowned and turned to the man, asking, "What?"

"Like eggs. Rotten eggs."

Paula sniffed as did Luke. "No, I don't smell it."

The man turned to Grace. "You. It's you. What are you?"

Grace stepped back, her chest filling with something hard. It obstructed her airway, and she reached up, clutching at her throat. "What... What have..." She couldn't talk.

"Grace?" Luke reached for her. "Grace, it's okay. Breathe for me, sweetheart." His arms enveloped her, but the fury on his face was directed at the man. "Get. Out. Get out now."

Panic wreathed Grace, because spots now appeared before her eyes. She wanted to breathe. Needed to. Any second now and she'd pass out. Her fingers clutched Luke's shirt and she was sure something tore. Grey edged her vision as she dropped down; only Luke's hold on her stopped her from hitting the floor.

Is this it? Is this how I die?

Paula stepped in between Luke and herself and the man. She obscured the view, and finally the pressure on Grace's chest started to release. Grace inhaled deeply, tears dribbling down her face.

Luke's hand cupped her cheek. "I was so scared, baby. What happened?"

Grace didn't have an answer and simply stared at the man holding her so tenderly.

The sound of the door closing had Luke raising his head. "He's not welcome here, Paula. Get rid of him. I won't have someone using magic in my home."

"Magic?" Grace queried.

"You were able to breathe once he couldn't see you, right? That's some kind of magic. I don't know what but..." Luke sighed, the sound ragged, and he closed his eyes.

Paula crouched down. "He said there was a smell. Like eggs. Only one type of creature I know of can do that." She glared at Luke who frowned.

"Demons."

~

LUKE KEPT Grace close and ordered Paula to meet him at the meadow. They'd drive down in his truck, but he'd be keeping a close eye on Francis, and under no circumstances would he allow the man within spitting distance of Grace.

She sat stiff and still beside him in the vehicle. He couldn't blame her. Francis had clearly done something, and it terrified him to think that she could have died there on his entrance floor.

"I have an amulet in the glove compartment, it's a protection seal amulet. I want you to put it on."

"You want me to wear an amulet?"

"Whatever Francis did, I won't let him do it again. It's in the glove compartment in a clear plastic box." He pointed to the small door in the dash. "Put it on."

She followed his instructions and slid the chain from the box.

The item itself was set with an iridescent gem. "Why do you carry...?"

"My grandmother gave it to me after my father died. She wanted to protect me, but I can't wear it, as it interferes with my work."

"But isn't it attuned to you?" Then she blinked. "And how do I even know that?" Wonder tinged her voice.

He glanced in her direction. "I don't know, but you do. And no, she bought it from a girl who had been given it by a friend. It's not attuned, so anyone can wear it. Even you. Especially you." They approached the edges of the wards, and he stopped the vehicle, letting it idle as he turned in her direction. "We're about to head out of the wards and I need to know you'll be safe. Please, put it on."

Grace opened her mouth, but he shook his head. "Don't argue. Please."

She followed his instructions. "Oh," she whispered. "That's odd. It's cooling me, like a wave of sensation."

"It's working?"

"I think so," she answered. "As I said, it's cooling me. Like it thinks I'm too warm and need a personal air conditioner."

He cupped her cheek. "I don't know how they work or feel when they're activated. I've never spoken about it with anyone who's worn one, but it's doing something from what you've just said. Now promise me you'll stay safe. Away from Francis. We'll do this as quickly as we can then head home."

She nodded.

He grimaced and wondered if that was enough of an answer. Anyway, he'd have to make do for now, and later he'd talk to Paula about what the hell Francis really was, so he could identify if it was a threat to Grace.

Inwardly fuming, Luke drove the distance to the open gate, where the wards ended, and into the meadow.

The sun was shining, the grass swaying, and the wildflowers nodded their heads as if welcoming him.

"It's very beautiful here," Grace breathed.

He smiled, because even after such a traumatic experience, like the one she'd had at the house, she could still appreciate the wonders of nature. The splendour of his home. It was humbling.

"One day, when we mate, this is where we'll celebrate."

He blinked, surprised by the words which appeared in his mind. He and his wolf rarely conversed like this.

"Because you rarely listen to me. But you should now."

"What?" The word escaped.

"Did you say something?" Grace asked.

He shook his head. *"What do you mean, I should now?"* Luke was sure his wolf was laughing at him.

"She's your mate, and you know she's in danger, otherwise you wouldn't have made her wear that amulet. Francis isn't your greatest problem though."

Stopping the vehicle, Luke looked around, surprised that he'd navigated next to Paula's car without even thinking.

"Good, you're here," she said with a false gaiety.

His gaze flicked to Francis who stood a little apart. He didn't like the man being on his property, but he'd have to suck it up for now. The sound of a distant engine rumbled, and they turned as Nate's four-wheel drive entered the meadow.

Paula drew closer. "You'll want to talk afterward?"

He turned a little so they could see each other clearly. "I will. But let's get this done."

Grace hunched against him, and he took her hand, while his sister glanced at the way their fingers entwined with a slight smile.

Once Nate had parked, he stalked over, nodded to Francis and Sienna before reaching for Paula, who kissed his cheek. The intimacy of the moment should have been uncomfortable, but for the first time Luke understood why it was more than a necessity to touch; it was two weres deeply committed to each other greeting their mates.

Nate turned to him, extending a hand, which Luke took. Then Nate smiled at Grace. "And this is...?"

"Tell him. Say: this is my mate."

"This is Grace. She's... staying with me." The words were less than he wanted to proclaim, but they wouldn't embarrass her. She didn't know or understand the depths of his attachment, and they didn't yet know why Francis would have done what he did. All they knew for sure was there was a heavy hex, there was a threat, and someone was looking for her.

He had no intention of endangering her.

Nate gave him a funny look.

"What?" Luke asked.

"I asked if she'd be attending the wedding," his friend and alpha clarified.

"Oh, yes, she will be. Paula?"

"Sure, I'll get her added to the list and make sure she's seated beside you." His sister grinned. "Grace, don't you just love this meadow? It's so pure and fresh."

Grace nodded in silence, and he wondered if it was too much, but she kept her counsel, though the pressure of her grip tightened.

CHAPTER

TWELVE

Grace couldn't say what it was that made her feel so uncomfortable. Nate, Paula's fiancé and their alpha, seemed nice, as did Sienna, but Grace didn't miss the dagger looks Francis kept shooting in her direction.

The amulet itched, and she tried hard to ignore it. She also knew Luke was aware of her discomfort, unlike the physical discomfort caused by Francis's proximity. She'd keep that knowledge to herself.

The meeting was over quickly enough, and Paula asked Nate if he could take Sienna and Francis back to their vehicles.

Nate frowned but agreed, but not before adding, "Then I'll come back. We've things to discuss. Pack matters."

Grace wasn't sure if that was quite accurate. She had a suspicion he had questions about her, why she was here, clinging to Luke for dear life, and what her history was.

She bit her lip and turned to Luke. In the just over a day since she'd met him—and really, that was all—he'd become essential to her. Not just because he'd protected her, and they'd made love—*had sex*, her brain corrected—and she was staying with him, but there was a connection. There'd been a subconscious click between them

—rather like puzzle pieces falling into place— which had grown stronger overnight.

Settling into the seat beside him, she remained silent. At least audibly, because her mind was spinning trying to make sense of it all.

I'm not a woman who needs someone to prop me up, to support me, so why do I feel like this? I can't afford to surrender myself to another person, and I won't endanger them. So why am I even considering all this?

Too many questions and no answers. Her attention shifted, watching as Luke drove with skill and care over the uneven and heavily wooded area, and soon they were parked in the garage again.

They climbed out and he came around to her. "Grace?"

"What?" She glanced at him, confused and frustrated because this wasn't her persona. She was strong. Independent. Self-sufficient.

"You're being very quiet."

"Maybe that's who I am?" she countered. Because did he really know her after twenty-four hours?

"I've already ascertained you're not a chatterbox, but I also know you ask questions. And you haven't asked anything since Francis's arrival. Are you alright?"

She opened her mouth to answer 'I'm fine,' but closed it again. Lying wasn't her style. "I'm thinking, Luke."

The door to the garage opened and Paula stalked in. "Right, what's going on then?"

Grace shrank back, because this was between brother and sister in her mind. Except, Luke grabbed her hand and hauled her close.

"What the hell is Francis?" Luke demanded.

Paula shook her head, either unable or unwilling to answer him. He knew Paula and Francis were friends, but whether she felt she needed to keep his confidence or whatever, he—and Grace—deserved to know.

The sound of Nate's four-wheel drive sedan driving up filled the air, and Grace suspected he'd driven swiftly, dropped off his passengers beyond the ward, where she guessed they'd parked, and hurried back.

Luke's gaze watched the approaching vehicle. "We should go into the lounge, because I have questions and I need answers."

He towed Grace and Paula followed, leaving the door open so Nate clearly would know to enter.

In the lounge, Grace headed for an armchair, but Luke stopped her, tugged her to the two-seater sofa, and settled her beside him. She blushed but remained quiet.

Nate entered the room, and he and Paula settled into the armchairs. "So, Luke, what the hell is going on?"

Luke tensed beside her, and Grace absently rubbed the hand holding hers with her thumb, and he relaxed, turning to smile at her. "Grace is a case and... more."

The words startled Grace. She was a case, she'd known that, but more? "Uh...?"

"My wolf talks to me," he said, speaking softly.

Paula and Nate's eyes widened. "He didn't before, did he? So what's changed?"

Luke gave an audible gulp, and Grace stared at him. *What the hell is going on?*

"My wolf and I are one, but we have a kind of agreement. He doesn't bother me or talk unless I'm in wolf form. But since Grace arrived on the scene, he does. He's told me she's my..." He winced and looked at her. "My mate."

"What?" She tugged her hand free and surged up. "Your mate? I don't think so, Luke. I'm sure that can't be right. He's probably confused. I mean, the sex was great..." She broke off then, aware of what she'd just revealed to the other two sitting there. "I need to get out of here," she muttered and stalked toward the hall.

"Grace? Please wait and hear me out," he called, but she shook her head and entered the bedroom.

~

"THAT'S one way to make a declaration," Paula stated with a grimace. "But it lacks finesse or romance."

Luke rose, scrubbing his hands over his face. "I've truly fucked that up," he muttered.

"Just a little," Paula responded.

"So, he's fallen for this woman—" Nate sounded confused.

"Francis attacked her. Mentally or magically, or something. Sniffed her and said he smelt eggs. *Sulphur.* So, brother of mine, what the hell is going on?"

Luke shook his head, trying to unravel his thoughts. "Paula is right. Francis did attack her, but I don't smell sulphur, and there's more. She's been hexed. A hex Thea can't unravel."

"Crap," Nate said. "She's the strongest witch in the region."

"Yeah," Luke replied, dragging his hands away. "Someone is looking for her, and we don't know why. She's running from someone who I think wants to hurt her, I've got a client directing this from overseas through a third party also overseas. As a child, Grace was found injured and alone, and she doesn't remember anything before then. That pretty much sums most of it up."

Nate stared at him. "Who's your contact?"

"David Tudor for the American wolf pack."

"Shit," he muttered.

"Why? What do you know?" Luke settled back in the seat he'd recently vacated.

"David Tudor is a wolf, true, but he's well-connected. Like very well. His sister and his cousin are both life partners of senior vampires. They report directly to Cressida. David himself was a '*Yeux Secondes*' or second eye to a vampire master, and his wife, Genevieve, is a wolf. But she has some connection to Padraic O'Shaunessy, the most senior leprechaun known to humanity."

"Oh." There didn't appear to be much else to say.

"So, whoever Grace is, she's attracted high-level interest," Paula concluded.

"Why are they looking for her?" Nate asked.

"That wasn't clear in the file. Just that she needed to be brought in, kept safe, and contact made when we found her." Luke sighed and closed his eyes.

"You haven't told her much, have you?" Paula asked.

"No. I offered to help her find out who she was first, so we could work out why they were looking for her."

"You need to make contact, Luke. Whatever we're dealing with is dangerous, and we can't endanger the pack." Nate's pronouncement had Luke's eyes snapping open.

"She's my mate," he argued.

Nate nodded. "I know. David Tudor is very astute. If he was hunting her to destroy, he'd have told you."

"And you know this how?" Luke challenged.

"After the fracturing, he was an envoy sent to assist, then with the vampire attacks on houses, I met him a few more times. He was part of the assistance crew to help with rebuilding nests who were attacked. As I said, he's well-connected and well-respected."

Luke wasn't sure about that, he didn't usually keep abreast of nest politics nor the other world as much as he likely should, relying on his assistants for that kind of information. And, not having met the man, he had to trust Nate's assessment. Not just because Nate was his alpha, but he was also an honest and fair man with an intuition that had proved trustworthy time and again.

"Alright, so I contact him. Later. For now, what the hell is Francis, Paula?"

She winced. "He's an elemental mage. But his mother was killed by a demon, so he's very attuned to them."

Luke snorted. "Mage? He's not welcome here again, sis. I don't care what you do, but he does not step foot on my property."

She nodded, eyes downcast. "I won't put your mate in danger, Luke. We won't lose another because of something I've allowed."

Luke sighed. "Father's death wasn't anyone's fault."

She shook her head. "That's not true, and you know it. I was there when it happened. I saw..." Paula cleared her throat, while Nate rubbed her arm. "Grace's safety is paramount now. But you're going to have to talk to her, because you currently have a very angry mate."

He nodded. "I know. Nate, I'll contact David later today, and I'll get Thea to come reinforce the wards too."

"You'll need to talk to Mum too, because once I add Grace's name to the list and amend the seating layout, she'll know. Then there'll be no stopping her." Paula sighed. "The timing does suck though."

"I'll ring her later today. Before two, I promise, just give me that much time?"

Paula nodded and rose. "We'll leave you to it then." She crooked her finger to her fiancé who also rose.

"Good luck," Nate muttered, then they left.

CHAPTER

THIRTEEN

Grace stomped around the room. She should leave. "I hate it when people keep secrets," she growled.

But honesty was something she'd always clung to, and in this case, the knowledge that after only twenty-four hours of time together Luke had already decided they were mates?

"I just don't know enough about weres and mating and all that. How the hell am I supposed to know if he's telling the truth?"

Throwing up her hands as she paced in a circle, she looked to the ceiling, stopped, then let her arms slide down. Maybe he was confusing sex and love?

She shook her head. If that was all it was, surely his sister Paula would have called him on that. Maybe? *What the hell do I know about families though? Mine wasn't some picture-perfect family on a greeting card.*

The soft knocking on the door had her spinning around. "Can I come in?" Luke's voice echoed, and she sighed.

"Might as well," she muttered and reached for the knob, opening the door. "What?"

"We need to talk."

"No shit, Luke."

His eyes widened at her coarse language. "Come out to the verandah, and I'll grab us something to eat."

"Is this going to take a while?"

He shrugged and his shoulders slumped. "Please, Grace?"

"Why not," she answered with ill-grace. "After all, it's your place."

He sighed and led the way.

Settling at the table, she waited for him in silence, hating the loss of control at him hiding something so significant from her. The knowledge he claimed felt tenuous at best, muddied by the sexual connection. Hot though it had been, it had her questioning the 'mate' relationship he claimed they shared.

He carried out a tray piled with sandwiches, fruit, a jug of icy lemon water, and, she noted, doughnuts.

"I didn't bother with plates, unless you—"

"It's fine," she answered, grabbing the glasses on the tray and pouring drinks. "So, what do you want to tell me?"

"I didn't tell you about the mate thing because neither of us is ready for that. We've only just met. I didn't think you'd need the pressure, and neither did I expect things to move so quickly."

"As in last night?" She raised her brow.

"I don't... I mean, I'm not into casual encounters," he said. She stared at him, remembering this morning's uncomfortable chat about sex and weres. "But last night the need was there. You felt it too, didn't you?"

She sighed, because yes... yes, she had. "But what does that mean to anything?"

"Look, finding a mate, for us, is an individual thing. Sometimes we find them and just know, and other times our wolf does, and we find out later. With you, my wolf knew and he... The boundaries between what I want and what he wants merge sometimes. But that doesn't mean I'm going to let him decide a relationship between us. I didn't tell you when he let me know." Luke shrugged. "I didn't want to pressure you. But then Francis arrived."

"Yeah, and what was that all about?"

"He's an elemental mage and he's... When he mentioned sulphur there was only one outcome."

She held herself still, because this... The importance of what he said next was something she couldn't ignore. And she truly feared what he was about to say.

"Demon."

She blinked, hand stopping with a grape halfway to her mouth. "Demon? You think I'm a demon?"

"I don't know. But I have a contact. David Tudor." He watched her, as if hoping it was a name she recognised.

"I don't know anyone by that name." She slid the grape into her mouth and chewed, needing a moment.

"He's the man I need to contact next. He's got powerful connections."

Jitters started in her belly. "What if he wants to kill me? What if he's the one behind...?"

Luke sighed. "I don't think so. His connections are impeccable. He's connected to the vampires, the American were clans, and the leprechauns."

The last word stilled her. She swallowed. "Leprechauns? They're real?"

Luke nodded. "Just about everything, including nymphs, faeries, and dryads are too. Along with trolls, dwarves, and elves."

"Riiiiggghtt." She reached out, grabbing her glass and taking a deep gulp.

"It's a lot to take in."

"You're telling me," she muttered. "So, demons and angels too?"

"Gods and goddesses as well." He smiled. "But Nate knows David a little. He said if it was something to be worried about, we'd know."

"What else could it be?" She winced, realising how flippant that sounded.

"I don't know, Grace. That's why we need to contact him. And on that note, I also need to contact my mother."

Grace blinked. "Why?"

"Because you'll be attending the wedding. As my mate." He watched her, as if waiting for the words to sink in.

"What does that mean?"

"Now, you're family," he said. Once more Grace opened her mouth, but he held up a hand. "I'll tell her to give you space. You'll have to meet everyone, but we can make it easy on you. I'll also remind her she's not going to be making any announcements. I'm the head of the family, so it's my decision. There'll be parts of the ceremony where I'm busy, so I'll make sure she looks after you, makes sure you have a seat and are comfortable."

Tears pricked her eyes, because no one had ever done anything like that for her before. But maybe he was wrong? What if his mother detested her?

Another thought occurred. "Are you going to tell her what you think I am?"

He shook his head. "No. If and when that's determined beyond a doubt, we'll find a way to tell her. But for now, you're simply my mate and due every respect accorded to a senior member of the family."

CHAPTER

FOURTEEN

Checking the time, Luke palmed his phone, while Grace watched, her face pale and lips pursed tight. She'd made it clear that while she understood the necessity to make the contact, she didn't like it.

He dialled the number and waited for an answer.

"David Tudor here." The answer was scratchy, reminding Luke that the man he was talking to was on the other side of the world.

"Luke Jones, from Freedmont, Jones, and McIntosh in Brisbane. I'm handling your case."

"Ah, Mr Jones, have you made progress?"

"I have," he replied. "I have Ms Cranston here beside me. But before we go any further, I am authorised to advise she is under the care of alpha Nate Davison." He waited and was surprised by the chuckle.

"How the hell did Nate get involved? He's a good alpha, but this is a mess he probably needs to be careful of," David cautioned.

"He's marrying my sister, Paula. They met Ms Cranston earlier today. I should also make you aware that she's my mate." He needed to make sure the man on the other side of the line understood that his concern, first and foremost, was Grace. He'd do nothing to put her in a position where she was at risk.

"Damn," David said. "Would you put her on speaker phone please?"

Grace's gaze connected with his and she nodded. "She already is."

"Ms Cranston, my father-in-law, Padraic O'Shaunessy, is tasked with tracking you down. He owes a debt to a highly placed demon who's underling is... related."

"Related to whom?" she queried, her voice wobbling a little.

Luke knew Grace was nervous, as her hands clenched together. He reached over, took a hand, and squeezed to let her know he was there to support her. *"We will always support her."*

"It's difficult to explain," David answered. "But what can you tell us of your early years?"

Grace grimaced, and Luke felt her frustration. "Not much. I was found by the side of the road. They think I was about ten. I don't remember anything before that though."

Luke noted she didn't tell him the rest and suspected she wasn't going to offer any information regarding the circumstances of her discovery unless and until she was ready.

"Has she been hexed?" David asked, and Luke was aware the question was aimed at him.

"Yes, I've had a witch come and they've determined it's a much stronger one than they've encountered before," Luke replied.

"It would have to be." The murmur was low, but not so much that Luke couldn't hear. "Can you send Ms Cranston to me? Perhaps you'd escort her?" David asked.

"No. I'm not in a position to leave until after Nate and Paula's mating, next weekend." Besides which, Grace wasn't going anywhere until Luke knew what they planned.

David sighed. "I'll come to you then. I'll have several in my entourage, but we'll make our own arrangements and let you know.

We'll stay at a nest locally, so as not to intrude. We understand mating ceremonies are sacred."

"Thank you. If you could send through your itinerary once it's organised?"

"Yes. Thank you, Mr Jones. I'll be in touch," David said, and the call ended.

"Oh man! Now what?" Grace muttered. "He's coming here to do what?"

Luke shook his head. "I don't know, but you'll be protected," he growled.

"I can't live in a bubble, Luke. I ran for years, hid on the ships and I told myself I was safe. I thought I'd thrown it off, but with that Francis character, and your Mr Tudor... I don't think that's the case at all. I need to live. To be normal." She blinked rapidly.

"We'll get to the bottom of this, but Nate and Paula's wedding is making it difficult to address some of these issues immediately."

She shook her head. "So, what? I hide out here? Doing nothing but twiddling my thumbs?"

"You do whatever you want, Grace. Cooking or crafts or reading or sleeping..."

He knew she felt hemmed in. Hell, it would be hard after spending years making decisions for yourself, to have to hand over control. Particularly when her actual life was hanging in the balance. *At least it won't be for long,* he thought, but didn't say the words out loud. She was already too stressed by the situation.

And he couldn't ignore the other tasks waiting. He still had his mother to ring, revelations to make. He nearly rolled his eyes, but stopped himself, because... well, that would be childish, right?

"We need to call my mother," he told Grace and saw the way her lips thinned.

"Maybe just tell her I'm a friend?"

He shook his head. "No can do. Mum's too insightful. She'll know. Besides, these things get around damn quick. If I don't tell her and she finds out…" He shook with a dose of dramatics, hoping she'd take the hint.

"Fine, whatever."

He frowned. "You don't want to tell my mum, or you don't want to make it official or…?"

She sighed, shoulders slumping. "I honestly don't know. It's not like I've ever been in a situation like this before."

"No, likely not," he replied. He brought up his mother's contact card on his phone and dialled. "Hi, Mum," he got out before she could speak.

"Luca! Where have you been? Neither Paula or Nate will tell me what's happening apart from the wedding is shifted to the meadow."

"Yeah, about the wedding, I'm happy to have it here, but just in the back meadow, so that keeps the house private. But I'm making a request," he hedged, his gaze on Grace.

Silence stretched. "What? A request? What could you possibly want—?"

He closed his eyes. "I'm not going to attend alone."

"What? Luca?" His mother sounded distracted and more than a little frustrated.

"I'm bringing my mate."

Seconds of silence passed. Then a squeal. "Your mate? Luca? Who is she? Do I know her?" Excitement rose in her voice, and he had to grip his hands together to contain his reaction—and noted that Grace had paled, her body curled as if ready to give in to the urge to flee.

"Slow down, Mum. No, you don't know her. Her name is Grace, and she's lovely."

"How do you know? Did you have a PI follow her? Check on her background? Who is her family? How old is she, and when can I meet her?"

It was a cascade of questions, all of which he wanted to avoid, but his mother was a determined woman. She'd keep asking until he answered.

"I know because my wolf told me. No, I haven't had her followed. Her family is not in the picture, and you'll meet her next weekend. But I have a favour to ask."

"Anything, Luca," she gushed, and he winced, looking to Grace.

"She's attending the wedding with me. Paula and Nate are adding her to the list, but I need you to make sure she's looked after during the ceremonial bits when I'm busy. Make sure she has somewhere to sit and isn't alone. Could you do that for me?"

"Oh, Luca," she cried. "Of course I will. When can I meet her? Don't make me wait until the mating ceremony!"

Luke sent a questioning glance to Grace who bit her lip and looked like a startled rabbit. "Grace?"

She shrugged. "I don't...?"

He sighed. "Later in the week, Mum. We'll arrange a dinner here."

"Come home, and I'll cook—"

He shook his head then realised she couldn't see him. "No. There are reasons that keep us at home, so you'll need to come here. We'll cook."

"But Luca, how can I welcome a new daughter if I can't cook for her?"

"Mum, honestly, it's easier if we stay here. I know you want to—"

"No. No, it's alright if you don't want my cooking. You're young and have your own way. That's alright. I can—"

Grace batted Luke's hand away, taking the phone. "No, we'll come to you, Mrs Jones," she said.

"No, Grace. You need to—"

"Luke, I don't want to upset her. So, organise a day and time, and we can head on over." Grace's face was pleading, and he shrugged, and she handed back the phone.

"I'll text you, Mum."

"Oh, Luca, I'm so pleased. Before the weekend would be good, because Paula and I are going over her last-minute appointments starting Monday, and I need to make sure all the plans are settled, the bedrooms cleaned out, and—"

"I love you, Mum, but I have to go," he broke through, hoping to calm her excitement.

When they'd hung up, Grace was watching him, biting her lip.

"What's wrong, Grace?"

"Should we have told her? I mean, what if it turns out..."

He understood what she was asking. "You are my mate. My wolf knows it, and so do I."

"But... What about love?"

"What about it? My wolf already adores you, and I'd die for you."

She blinked. "Oh." And she nodded before standing and leaving the room.

A sense of disquiet slid into him. *What did I say wrong?*

CHAPTER

FIFTEEN

G race settled onto the bed. She'd left Luke outside where they'd eaten. Why was she upset? After all, he'd said he'd die for her. Why wasn't that enough?

Besides, why was she even considering what he'd said as a fact? Sure, he'd said those things. Maybe he did believe them, but what was the reason *she* trusted him, because in truth, she did. She wasn't the kind of woman who'd blindly agree to things that impacted her. In the past, everything would require evidence before she could make decisions.

Then the call with his mother had pushed her to do something out of character. To plunge into not just a relationship, but a family.

She stood, paced a circle on the floor of the room, and tried to unravel the wild knot of her thoughts. After the tumult of the morning, meeting his sister and dealing with the man who'd done some kind of juju on her, she'd been off-balance.

"So, what the hell do I do now?" she asked herself.

She could just keep riding the wave, let him look after her. Meet his family and hide out until this David arrived.

"I could just leave, not tell him. Hide out. I can get the cash and

91

just go to ground." The thought was tempting, but she wasn't a coward. Besides, something intrinsic told her that would hurt both of them far too much to bear.

What other options were there?

Too much. Too much going on in my head. She strode to the bathroom, attended to the needs of her body, then splashed her face. Water flicked onto the mirror, and she looked up at herself, her visage rippling.

A face appeared; one she didn't know. A creature she couldn't define reached toward her, and Grace reared back, a cry lodging in her throat.

She reacted, grabbing a washcloth and swiping it over the mirror. The image disappeared, but her breathing was shallow, laboured as she stared at the glass. "What the hell...?"

None of this made any sense, and it wasn't anything she'd ever seen before.

Who or what...? She shook her head and stepped back and away from the vanity unit, before she might see anything else. The buzz of fear vibrated through her, and her legs felt like wet lettuce leaves.

Leaving the bathroom, she stumbled to the bedroom, and Luke was there, having crashed through the door.

"What's wrong?" His face was tight, eyes focused on her, lips flat. "I felt your distress..."

She shook her head. *He wouldn't believe me.* "I... It's nothing," she whispered

He stepped over to her and grabbed her upper arms. "Grace? Tell me."

Tears burned Grace's eyes, and she blinked them away.

His fingers bit deep. "What's got you terrified?" There was a growl in his voice and that was disconcerting on top of her fright at the visage which had appeared in the mirror.

"There was a face!" she wailed.

His gaze narrowed on the window. "Where?"

Mute, she simply shook her head.

"Where, Grace?" His demand was harsh.

"In the mirror!"

His nostrils flared. "Where?"

"In the bathroom. Luke, what's happening?"

He pushed her toward the bed, made sure she was perched there before he stalked into the bathroom.

The moments he was in there were long before he returned. "I need to talk to Thea. Come with me." When he reached out, she took his hand, and he noticed the shaking. "Damn it," he growled, reaching down to scoop her up against his chest. "Nothing will hurt you, Grace. I won't allow it. My wolf won't allow it either."

The wildness in Luke's eyes should have increased her terror, but it didn't. The bubble of fear which stole her ability to think receded. Not all the way, but enough to let her think. Nothing she knew had petrified her as much as what she'd seen in the mirror.

"What's happening, Luke? What was it?" If it was supernatural, and the evidence appeared to indicate it was, surely he'd know the what?

"I don't know, my love. But I won't let anything hurt you, you know that, don't you?"

She nodded, but was unsure why she was agreeing. His emotional response was telling. He was as at sea as she was.

In the lounge, he settled her on the chair. "I'm going to get my phone. Stay here," he said and strode out to where they'd had lunch. When he returned, it was with the phone to his ear. "Thanks for answering, Thea."

Grace couldn't hear what was being said by the woman on the other end of the connection, but she saw the darkening of his features as he nodded.

"I know. No, something happened. She saw a face in the mirror, and she's terrified."

He looked to her, held out a hand while settling on the seat beside her. The warmth of his touch beat back the chill which filled her bones.

"Yeah, now would be good." He glanced at Grace, then concluded the call with, "See you soon."

As he disconnected the call, he sighed, pulling his fingers through his hair.

"She'll be here soon," he said, "but she's got a few calls to make first."

Grace turned away, looking out toward the road. "If the danger is too much—"

He turned so that they were on eye level. "No way. You're not going anywhere."

Blinking, Grace considered the man before her, and while her ire rose, she also understood. His very nature was to protect. "You can't tell me what to do, Luke. I'm an adult, capable of thinking for myself." He needed to understand that. She had no intention of giving up control of her life even in the most fraught of circumstances.

"I won't let you get hurt."

Unable to help herself, Grace grinned. "Do you honestly think I'm going to put myself in a position where I would be hurt? I'm just thinking that the danger can't and shouldn't overshadow your sister's wedding."

She reached out and cupped Luke's cheek, wondering at the instant connection between them. The depth of their bond. Whether caused by the mating bond, or something else, she felt it. Maybe not the way he did, but like there was a tether between them. He wanted to protect her, and she wanted to be with him. He made her feel whole.

"What's going on in your head?" he muttered. "I know you're thinking, but I can't divine it."

A small laugh escaped. "I'm not sure you'd want to. I'm a jumbled mess right now."

He growled. "I want to know everything about you. Me and my wolf."

She seized on his words. "Does he... Does he have a distinct personality?"

"Oh yeah," Luke answered. "He's possessive, a hunter who needs what he's sure is his. You."

"So, it's like having a second person in your skin?"

Luke cocked his head. "A little." He rose, tugging her up with him. "I want to show you who he is, but not now. Right now, I need to kiss you."

His lips found hers, and the heat exploded between them. She wrapped her arms around the back of his neck, letting his heady scent and taste fill her. Inside, the molten lava licked at her, demanding more, that she strip him and let their bodies entwine. The puckering of her nipples and the sudden melting in her belly left her feeling empty and wanting.

All too soon though, he pulled away. "Gods, I don't think I'll ever get used to how good you feel and how you make me hungry," he muttered, resting his forehead against hers.

The knock on the door broke through the cocoon around them.

"That'll be Thea," he said.

She waited as Luke trudged to the door, returning moments later with the woman she'd met before.

"Hello, Grace. It's nice to see you again," Thea said, and Grace replied affirmatively.

"So, do you know anything?" Luke's query cut through the air, and Thea grimaced.

"A little. But none of it is what I'd call good. It revolves around demonology." Thea waited, as if expecting some kind of outburst, but Grace just stared at the woman.

"Demonology? I... What?" Luke growled.

"Don't shoot the messenger, but some cursory research leads me to believe that demons are involved. Certain demons, particularly strong ones, can use their powers to make mirrors like visual portals. They can't come through, or at least that's what I've found out, but members of the coven are continuing the research for me." Thea slumped down into one of the seats.

"Why would a demon be looking through a mirror portal in my spare room?" Luke sounded bewildered, but suddenly Grace connected the dots.

"To find me," she croaked.

Thea nodded while Luke's gaze was surprised.

"You know why?" he demanded.

"No, but it makes sense. The attack by Francis, my collapse when Thea was here last. It all seems super coincidental otherwise, doesn't it?"

LUKE HATED the defeat infusing Grace's words. She thought she was at fault. "No, it's not your fault."

Her eyes displayed her misery when she glanced up at him. "Sure it was. It's all my fault. You never had to deal with issues like this before. I should leave..."

He reached out and manacled her wrist with his hand so she wouldn't rise and leave. "You aren't going anywhere until we find out what's going on."

"I agree," Thea stated. "If demons are involved, we need to be sure, Grace. I can give you an amulet to keep the demons at bay, though I see you have one already. May I look at it?"

"It's a protection seal," Luke said as Grace slid it off and handed it over to Thea.

She inspected it and nodded. "Yes, but it's not been charged in a long time. The power is weak. But to be honest, that won't stop them looking for a weak point to enter your home, Luke. When I say the demon has to be powerful, I do mean exceptionally powerful."

"I wonder if Padraic O'Shaunessy knows anything..."

"O'Shaunessy. The Irish leprechaun?" Thea's face paled.

Luke grunted his agreement, while nodding.

"Well, that makes things a little clearer. Yes. If O'Shaunessy is looking for you, you best make contact as soon as possible. He has contacts to the strongest of the demon world. In fact, his wife is part demon."

Luke stared at the witch. "Part demon?"

"Yes, but not all demons are evil—you know that, right?" Thea's question sounded amused, but there was nothing amusing about the situation.

"No?" Grace asked. "Then all the stories are wrong."

"No." Thea shook her head. "Some of them are really bad. Like vicious, hateful creatures that want to destroy the world. But some are not. From what I hear, there's a war going on between the two camps. Anyway, when O'Shaunessy's wife was abducted by one, it was others who worked with the various creatures massed to defeat the evil demons. She came back, though it was touch and go for a while whether she'd survive. But I did hear that O'Shaunessy is working with some to rebalance what's going on in the demon world."

Luke shook his head. Evil demons. Not bad demons. How had he missed all these goings on? "So, what do you suggest then?"

Thea sighed. "None of this is straightforward, Luke. We should charge the protection seal, but we need help."

"I've got David Tudor and—"

She nodded. "That's an excellent starting point, but you should check if O'Shaunessy is coming too. You do know David Tudor's wife is O'Shaunessy's daughter, don't you?"

He frowned. "Yeah. Which is confusing, because isn't Tudor a wolf?"

She laughed. "He is, but his wife is a leprechaun-wolf hybrid." She held up a hand. "Don't ask me how that works, because until recently I would have said it wasn't possible. But there are prophecies that suggest things are predestined to address issues in our world, so who am I to argue with that? But for the short-term, you need to stay here, Grace. We need Tudor to arrive and hopefully bring O'Shaunessy with whoever is travelling."

"But the wedding is next weekend," he argued.

"You're going to have to take care then. We could ward—"

He shook his head. "Not an option," he growled.

"Then we need to get the amulet charged up ahead of the event. Until then, Grace needs to stay here."

CHAPTER
SIXTEEN

Grace didn't like being the object of the discussion, particularly when she had nothing useful to offer. So by the time Thea left, she was thoroughly out of sorts.

She moved to the kitchen, planning to grab a drink, and Luke followed her.

"I know you're upset about the plan I laid out," he said.

Her shoulders tensed at his words. "It's not a plan, Luke. What you're suggesting is I hide. I've had enough of hiding. I've done it for years, and you know that."

Luke looked surprised when she rounded the counter to stare at him.

"But I don't get what's wrong," he said. "We hunker down here, and when they arrive, we can—"

"No, Luke." She spoke quietly, needing him to understand and knowing that being loud wasn't the answer. "I don't want to hide. This isn't what I think is the best outcome for me."

"All I want to do is keep you safe."

She nodded, holding onto her temper. "Yes, I get that, but

honestly don't you think that should be up to me? I mean, would I ask you to stay here without even consulting you?"

He stared at her blankly. "What?"

"Luke, we've only known each other a few days, right? You insist that we're mated, and I don't know if that's right. What I do know is it's all moved so fast, and we don't really know each other." She waited for him to understand.

"Grace, you need to believe me, I won't put you at risk." He reached for her, but she shook her head.

"Look, let me think, okay?" She turned and marched onto the verandah, needing air and time to think.

A mob of kangaroos were at the edge of the backyard, and on a whim, she headed for the stairs. Hurrying down, she moved one step after another, slid on a stair.

"Argh!"

She slid, leg beneath her. A loud crack filled the air. She screamed as pain bloomed.

Then the world turned black.

~

LUKE HEARD the scream and he bolted, terror shooting through his veins.

"Must protect. Save."

His inner wolf was fighting to break out, to destroy anything and anyone that might try to hurt Grace. At the top of the steps, Luke looked down. *"Fuck!* Grace! *Grace!"*

She was slumped at the bottom of the stairs, one leg caught between the treads, but it was immediately clear she'd broken her leg.

He jumped, thanking the gods for his athletic ability which came with his wolf, checking her breathing. Then, with shaking hands, he called the clinic.

Almost immediately the physician's reception answered.

"It's Luke Jones. One of my guests fell, and she's... She's broken her leg and is unconscious."

"Wait, Luke. Give me some details and I'll dispatch the ambulance to your location. Where are you now?"

He gave his address, directing them to the back steps, but the questions asked were more difficult to answer. He didn't know of any underlying medical conditions, nor did he know if she had any kind of medical insurance. "I'll cover any costs," he growled, his wolf becoming more furious by the moment.

He checked her again and was thankful on one level that she wasn't awake to feel the pain he was sure she'd endure, but on the other hand, he was petrified that she'd injured something else. Something he couldn't see. There was no way he should move her, in case there was a neck or back injury.

Moments ticked by as the woman on the other end of the line spoke to him, soothing him, and he guessed it was to keep him focused.

Footsteps broke through the veil surrounding him, and he looked up to see two men he knew hauling a stretcher behind them. "Luke, let us in so we can check her."

Davey, a were-tiger, hunched down beside him as Corey, another were he didn't know well, was unpacking medical equipment, no doubt in preparation for attending to Grace then moving her.

Luke rose, unsteady, and stepped back, not wanting to, but knowing he had nothing to offer in the circumstances.

The men were capable, unflappable, and gently checked Grace's neck and head, applying a collar brace. "Just in case," Davey said before sliding a board beneath her back. "We'll take every care, Luke."

He nodded, standing to attention, ready to pounce if he needed to. His wolf was so close to the surface, affecting his vision, while claws peeked out from his fingers.

"You'll want to come with us?" Corey's question had him

nodding. "And what's your connection?" Corey asked. "We need to gather as much information as possible."

"She's my mate," Luke answered, nausea rising.

The two men lifted her carefully, and Luke could clearly see the outline of the injury. Her leg was swollen and red where they'd cut away at the jeans she'd worn.

"We'll take her the long way and meet you at the front," Davey said, and Luke nodded before bounding up the stairs to gather his phone and wallet. His keys were shoved into his pocket, and he pushed in the locking knob before closing the doors behind him as he left the house.

The stretcher was already loaded and inside he could see Grace's white face.

"She'll be fine soon, Luke. We'll get her to the clinic and the docs will do their thing. Wait and see," Davey said, clapping Luke on the shoulder then indicating he should take a seat to the side.

LAYERS of grey cotton wool settled on her brain. Trying to open her eyes, Grace felt the mad ache in her skull.

Her mouth felt like someone had tipped a ton of sawdust into it, and she nearly choked trying to swallow. "Water," she muttered, keeping her eyes shut.

"Thank the Gods," a voice to the side of her said. "I thought you'd never wake. Here. Have a sip, but only a sip for now." A straw was slid against her mouth, and she sipped, feeling the water sliding over her tongue and down her throat.

"Luke?" she whispered.

"Yeah."

"What happened to me?" She remembered leaving the room, but the rest was a blank slate.

"You went outside and must have slid on the steps. I found you unconscious, and you've broken your leg."

"I can't feel my leg," she growled.

"They took you into surgery and reset your leg, under an anaesthetic. Damn it, Grace, you could have died." His voice faltered. "I would have lost you almost before we could begin."

She reached out, took his hand. Even in her woozy state she recognised that he was shaking. "But I didn't. When can I go home?"

"Maybe tomorrow. They need to keep an eye on you. How's the head?" He carefully pushed a strand of hair from her face.

"Hurts like the devil," she answered then grimaced. "Not sure I meant that quite as it came out," she moaned. "I'm tired, Luke. Maybe I should sleep." She moved, restless, and heard him moving. She opened her eyes, noting the blanket he was pulling over his lap as he settled in the recliner seat beside the bed. "You should go home, Luke."

"No. I'll stay here with you, love. You're never going to be left alone again."

EVEN NOW, hours on, Luke felt the burning rise of vomit in his throat, sour and hot. For a second, he'd been sure Grace was dead. He barely remembered jumping over the railings, only the fear which seized him and almost tore his chest open.

She lay in the bed, her face pale, and he could almost swear she was dead. The *beep beep* of the monitors reminded him she wasn't though. Thea had met him at the clinic and had explained rapidly that the amulet she wore mustn't be removed, something the clinic staff fought him over.

"It has to come off. We have to prep her for surgery," the intern had explained.

"It can't. She's too open already when awake to demonic forces, and if she's under anaesthetic, it's going to be worse," Thea said.

"I won't consent to the removal," Luke added, his stance belligerent, hands on hips and chin thrust forward.

"But..." the intern sputtered as the surgeon appeared at his shoulder.

"What's going on?" he demanded. "We need to get her into surgery as quickly as possible."

"The patient has been attacked and demons are trying to get her under their control. The amulet she wears is the only protection she has right now," Luke told the surgeon.

"They did this?" The intern pointed to her leg.

"No, she fell down the stairs. Look, can we hurry this up a bit?" Luke growled.

"She's your mate then?" the surgeon asked, understanding the situation and Luke's jumpiness.

Luke nodded.

"The amulet can stay. We're simply resetting the leg, then we'll put on a cast. It's just better, given the severity, that we do it while she's unconscious," the surgeon explained. "We'll update you once we're done and she's in recovery."

The waiting room had been small, with uncomfortable chairs, and he still felt as if he was wedged into the seat. Thankfully, he was now sitting in the comfortable recliner in Grace's private room. His eyes burned and his head ached, and he closed his eyes, not really tired, yet somehow bone-weary.

His phone beeped and he cursed, answering quickly.

"What's happened?" His sister Paula had clearly already heard about the ambulance visiting his house. "Is it you or Grace that's hurt?"

"It's Grace. She fell on the back step, knocked herself out and broke her leg." He rubbed his hand over his eyes.

"I've told you about those steps before, Luke. They're dangerous. You'll need to haul them out and replace them with something safe before you and Grace have kids." She softened her words, "I'm really sorry to hear that she's hurt though. She'll be fine?"

His gaze danced in the direction of the woman on the bed beside him. "Yeah, and I'll organise a builder as soon as we get this mess under control."

"How about I get the pack's builders to swing over and write up a quote," Paula offered. "At least then that will be one less issue you need to worry about."

He sighed. "That would be great. Also, can I get you to pick me up in the morning? I'll get Mum to come in and stay with Grace while I head home and get my car. They're talking about releasing her then, so long as the concussion isn't too bad."

"Where are you now?"

"I'm here, in the room with her. She's asleep—"

"They're letting her sleep? I thought possible concussions meant they had to stay awake. Is that the best option?"

He sighed at Paula's concern. "I asked. They said since she's already woken once, and she's not showing any alarming signs, that they'll let her sleep and check in on her every couple of hours."

"Okay then, I'll swing by in the morning around eight or eight-thirty."

He thanked her then ended the call, settling further down into the seat, wriggling his bum and sighing. *A long night ahead, but at least I'll be here.* His wolf agreed sleepily, and Luke decided he should sleep.

CHAPTER

SEVENTEEN

Waking in the morning, Grace felt the pain radiating from her leg; it left her gritting her teeth while she curled her fingers into the material of the sheet. She'd refused any pain relievers at four o'clock, and now at seven she regretted that.

"You're awake," Luke said near her ear.

"What are you doing here?" There was a bite in her voice, but her discomfort outweighed the need to be sweet.

"I stayed with you in case you needed me or in case something else happened."

Luke's eyes were shadowed and on his chin was the evidence of a long and broken night. Stubble which her fingers itched to touch. *What the fuck is wrong with me?*

She shifted and groaned.

"You need pain meds? The nurse said you didn't want any earlier. I can grab one of the—"

"No, but I want a shower, I want to get clean, and most of all, I want to go home." The words escaped in a rush, and she didn't miss the half-grin he quickly contained at her complaints.

"Home, hmm?"

She rolled her eyes, because why was he being so difficult?

"I'm going to go home, grab you some fresh clothes, and bring the car back so I can take you home. Then, if you want, you can settle in the lounge or on the verandah. Whatever you want, and I'll be your slave."

"Slave, huh? I'm not sure you're terribly suited to wearing a lap-lap and bowing and kowtowing to me. But hey, if that's the benefit of this," she said through gritted teeth, because she was trying to ignore the twin needs of her body—bathroom and escaping the pain.

"So, what do you need?" He leaned in. "Shall I get some naughty food for you on the way over or wait 'til we're going home?"

"I'd like to go to the bathroom, if at all possible," she muttered just as the nurse walked in, carrying a tray and large piece of footwear in her hands, and settled the items on a shelf.

"Okay, you..." the nurse said, pointing at Luke, "need to leave the room for a while."

He stood, raising his hands. "I'll be back soon. Mum is due here any tick of the clock, and she'll look after you."

He left before the nurse could usher him out of the room. "Well now, he's a bit intense, isn't he? Let's get you up and into the chair. The doctor wants you moving quickly. So I've brought you a moon-boot, and it's so you." She grinned. "I'll grab you some crutches too. Have you ever used them before?"

She blushed and the nurse waited for her to explain her need. "I need the bathroom," Grace whispered.

"Ah." The nurse nodded. "I have just the thing." She reached into a cupboard and whipped out a bedpan. "Until we're ready to move you, we'll need to struggle along with this." She raised the head of the bed. "Ready?"

Embarrassment coursed through Grace, but she was desperate to relieve herself, so she used the item. Once the nurse had disappeared to dispose of the contents, Grace groaned. "This totally sucks."

"Yes, it really does," the nurse said as she re-entered the room with two metal crutches in hand. "So, have you used crutches before?"

Grace nodded. "A long time ago, but yes. I think I remember how."

The nurse pulled aside the bed clothes. "Slide on over, but take it slow."

As Grace started to move, pain zinged again. "Ahhh..."

"Hmm, you didn't take your pain meds at four, did you? Let me nip out and grab some, then we'll give it a minute to kick in. You can have your breakfast then too."

She moved and Grace waited, feeling very sorry for herself as her leg throbbed.

The nurse bustled back in soon with a tiny, white paper cup. "Hold out your hand," she said and placed the cup into Grace's hand.

Grace popped the pills into her mouth and took the drink she was offered to wash them down.

"Now, here's your breakfast," she said and grabbed the waiting tray of food. "And I'll get everything ready for you to move into the seat. I want to be sure those tablets have kicked in before we try you on the crutches."

Grace ate slowly. Hospital food hadn't improved any, she noted. Even if it was a private room. The yoghurt was tangy but no fruit, the muesli serve was contained in a tiny bowl, and the small portion of milk in an individual bottle. The coffee was tepid.

Even so, she ate it all, realising she hadn't eaten for over eighteen hours, and slowly the pain in her leg receded to a dull ache.

A woman bustled into her room, looking about thirty, with lush, dark hair and the same eyes as Luke. "Darling! Luke had me come over after he told me about your accident. Now you sit back, and Nurse Leuring and I will get you up and going. When Luke comes back with fresh clothes, you can have a shower and you'll begin to feel a little better."

The woman unloaded take-away coffee and a bakery bag onto

the tray, then slid an oversize bag onto the seat where Luke had spent the night.

"I... Um..."

She smiled at Grace and leaned in to kiss her on the cheek. "I'm Mama, Luke's mum. All the partners and boyfriends and girlfriends call me Mama, and so will you, sweetie. And aren't you just the prettiest girl ever!"

It was downright overwhelming, though Grace could feel the honest welcome in Mama's voice. So rather than shy away, she pushed aside her natural reticence. "Thank you, Mama."

"Good. Now, I brought you a blueberry Danish. I wasn't sure what you'd prefer, but you need feeding up. Oh, and Luke said you like coffee, so I got a mocha latte. I hope that's okay?"

"That's incredibly kind of you," she said, tears pricking her eyes.

"It's nothing. You're my daughter now, and we Joneses look after our own. If only my husband, Teddy, was still here. I know he'd love you. English to a fault he was," she said, sliding into the recliner after pushing her bag to the floor. "Much to the dismay of my own mama, who wanted me to find a good Italian boy, but love can't be foresworn, and neither can the pull of the mate."

Grace blinked. "You're a were too?"

The woman nodded. "Yes, a black wolf, unlike my Teddy, who was the most marvellous silver, and Luke has inherited both our genes. Black shot with silver. But of course, you've seen...?"

Shaking her head, Grace blurted out, "No, I haven't."

"Ah, then you have a treat coming. Anyway, eat up, dear. Don't let me interrupt you. The food here is better than most hospitals, but still bland and almost tasteless."

Grace coughed on a crumb, and though Mama rose to pat her back, she shook her head, sipped on the coffee. "I'm fine. Just... did Luke tell you what I do? For a living?"

"No, dear. We've barely talked about anything important. What do you do?"

Smiling at Luke's mother, she answered, "I'm a chef. I've worked on boats for years and was head chef on a long-haul freighter."

"Oh! That's wonderful. I'm terrible in the kitchen, just ask Luke and Paula. Teddy did most of the cooking when they were young, then Luca and Paola—yes, that's Luke and Paula—took over the kitchen. My youngest now cook. But maybe you could give me some pointers?" She smiled conspiratorially as the nurse re-entered the room.

"Alright, Grace. We need to get you up and mobile."

The nurse started to slide the boot onto her leg, and though it was cumbersome, Grace understood its necessity. Then she began the ungainly slide toward the edge of the bed, and while it really was uncomfortable, and the pain was present, the sharp edge was dulled. Soon she was leaning heavily on one crutch and scooping up the other under her armpit.

"You look to be balanced alright," the nurse said, examining her critically. "Can you make it to the door and back?"

Sucking up the discomfort, Grace clutched the sticks and hobbled her way forward, the injured leg doing no more than balancing her.

By the time she made it back to the bed, though, she was sweating.

"Excellent. Come settle in the chair, and I'll take your vitals in a few minutes. I need to check next door first." Then the nurse vacated the room, and it was Grace and Luke's mum again.

Luke entered the room, a bag in his arms. "Mum, you got here. Thanks. Grace, I've brought you toothpaste and toothbrush, some underwear, and a dress. I thought that would be easier with…" He stopped in the doorway. "You're up?"

Grace's hand moved to her hair, wondering if it was as wild as she expected.

"It's perfectly fine, sweetie. I have a brush and we'll sort that out after your shower," Luke's mother said.

CHAPTER

EIGHTEEN

Seeing Grace sitting upright in the chair and his mother hovering restored some of the sense of well-being which had been severely dented yesterday.

"A shower?" Grace queried.

She wasn't at her best, but upright was a gift in Luke's mind. Especially when he considered what he could be facing. A shiver rolled through his body, and he shoved the thought aside.

The nurse bustled back in. "Of course, but we'll usher everyone out and get you set up. I've these bags to slide over your leg and a Velcro band to slide over the rubberised ends. Let's get you into the bathroom and settled in the shower chair."

The nurse took the bag from Luke. "Now, you two head out to the seats outside the door while Grace and I get acquainted."

He didn't want to leave, but the nurse was insistent.

Luke led his mother out of the room and into the long, cold corridor. "Thanks for coming, Mum."

She patted Luke's cheek. "I'd be here, even if you didn't ask me to. The poor, little thing, she's all alone, or was. Now she's one of us, and we—"

"—look after our own," he finished his father's favourite mantra.

"Exactly. Now, when you get out of here, you take her home. Feed her properly—good, hearty, and healthy meals."

Luke smiled. "The kind you used to cook?"

His mother stared at him with a horrified expression. "No, like your father used to cook, Luca Jones."

"Yes, Mum," he answered with a smile.

LUKE'S FACE betrayed that he didn't want to leave. "Go on, the nurse and I won't be having any wild parties," Grace told Luke.

He stared at her then nodded and ushered his mother from the room.

"You're very lucky. A lot of men wouldn't want to be so involved in their partner's care. They think that's what we're paid to do and have no qualms passing over the tasks."

Grace settled in the small bathchair and waited as the nurse removed the moonboot, putting it up on a bench beside her clothes. "I guess."

"You're not comfortable with it?" The nurse spoke from behind her, sliding the band from her hair and fiddling with the bra straps before sliding it off Grace.

"It's new," she whispered.

"Ah." The nurse nodded. "Okay let's slide this up your leg." She moved quickly, well versed, it seemed to Grace, and soon the water was sliding over Grace's body.

"Oh, that feels better," she whispered.

Once they'd finished, the nurse assisted her to remove the bag and dry off before grabbing the underwear and crouching to slide it over Grace's feet and helping her to rise. She slid the crutches over her arms once a fresh bra was in place and helped her limp to the bench.

"Get the dress over your head, while I get the boot on you, then you can do your teeth."

Grace did, grabbing the three-quarter length dark blue dress, thankful the jersey material was kind and stretchy.

She rose to brush her teeth, taking the brush with a smile. She turned on the faucet and looked up. Sucked in a breath as a face appeared. A hand speared through the mirror.

She screamed and fell back, the nurse catching her and tugging her to the bench.

Grace's hand rose to grip the amulet... "My necklace," she screeched.

The door burst open, and Luke was there, scooping her up. "Where's your amulet?"

"I took her necklace off so she could shower," the cowering nurse answered.

Grace glanced to the mirror, and once more it was a flat, shiny surface. "It's gone," she breathed.

"I saw it," sputtered the nurse as Luke hunted through Grace's discarded clothes and found the leather thong with the charm and slid it over her head. "What was it?"

Grace shook in reaction. There'd been a malevolence in the face she'd seen, and those fingers and claws had reached for her. Not the nurse, but her!

The chill that surrounded her melted slowly as she stayed burrowed in Luke's arms.

He rose and carried her into the room and laid her on the bed, while his mother hovered by the door. "What's wrong?" Mama asked.

Luke shook his head. "We need to get her home."

"The doctor needs to see her first," the nurse squeaked.

"Then get them in here. I need to get her to safety," he muttered. "Otherwise, I can have our alpha contact the hospital director," Luke growled, and the nurse scurried out of the room.

"Don't... Don't scare her, Luke. She's just trying to make sure everything is done right," Grace croaked.

"Luca, you never speak to people like that," his mama remonstrated.

"Mum, normally I wouldn't, but this is about Grace's safety. It's the reason we weren't coming to you. She's at risk when she's not behind the wards, and until our contacts from America arrive, we don't really know what we're dealing with."

Mama's stance changed, and she pulled herself up to full height, her gaze narrowing. "She's in danger?"

Luke nodded and Grace waited, breath held.

"Yes," he answered.

"That does not happen to members of the Jones family," Mama growled, nails elongating as the door opened and both the nurse and a doctor entered the room.

"What's going on? The nurse just informed me that you intend taking the patient before—" he blustered.

"Grace is at risk. She needs to be out of here now," Luke answered, his voice deep and dark.

"I will be making my rounds in an hour..."

Luke shook his head. "She won't be here then. Either you sign her release now, or we leave without it."

The doctor huffed and puffed but turned to the nurse. "Have you checked to see if she can use the crutches?"

"Yes, doctor," the nurse answered.

"Pass me her chart," he said and scanned it. "Fine." He scrawled his signature on the sheet. "I'll arrange her prescription for pain relief, and she'll need to return in ten days for a check-up." He looked at Grace, aiming the words to her, "If there's any swelling, loss of sensation or numbness, pain continuing after elevation and rest, etcetera, then you should make contact with the clinic. The nurse will give you a leaflet detailing the do's and don'ts for fracture care." Then he spun on his feet and left the room.

The nurse turned to Grace. "I'll get your prescription and the leaflet, and I'll be back in a few minutes."

"Mum, would you collect Grace's things from the bathroom?"

Waiting until his mum had left the room, Luke pressed a kiss to Grace's forehead. "I'm so sorry that happened. You were supposed to keep the amulet on. I explained all that when you were admitted yesterday."

Fury spiked within him. He'd told them, and clearly, they'd missed the importance of the item. It also meant that they hadn't passed the information to other staff, a gross oversight for a clinic that cared for a wide variety of paranormal patients.

Grace passed the amulet to him, and he slid it around her neck.

Her fingers gripped his upper arm. "It's okay, Luke. I'm fine."

"But you nearly weren't, and that's not okay. What if they'd pulled you through to the demon realm? The nurses and doctors have a duty of care, and I warned them that this could happen. Thea told me about the dangers that Padraic O'Shaunessy's wife faced, not via this avenue, but using a portal."

Grace shook again in his arms, not the wild tremors she'd exhibited before, but enough that he held her close until they passed. "I don't want this, Luke. I haven't done anything to cause this or... Is this because of whoever is looking for me, do you think?" She sounded so plaintive that it almost broke him. He had to breathe through his own distress, because he refused to add to hers.

"I think it's likely, Grace. But the sooner we get you home, the better. I rang Thea and she's checking some information for us, looking for a way to deal with the danger until David arrives." And he'd make sure that Grace wore that bloody amulet even when she was in his own home.

"And when is this likely to happen?" she demanded.

He shook his head. "I'll send a message to him as soon as we get home, my love."

"Then get me out of here," she pleaded, and he nodded as his mother returned to the room.

"Absolutely." He looked over his shoulder and asked, "Mum, can you go see how much longer? Hurry the nurse."

His mother left the room carrying the bag of underwear and the shirt. He didn't know where the shoes went and frankly didn't care either, because all he cared about was that Grace was safe and well.

He already carried enough guilt that she'd been injured while with him.

When the nurse trundled a wheelchair into the room, he felt the loosening of the knot that had formed in his chest. He lowered Grace into the chair, making sure she had the crutches. His mother held a bag, which he guessed included anything they needed.

"In the pack there's the prescription you can get filled at your local pharmacy. I've included information concerning those medications," the nurse said. "I've also added the physio exercises sheet that we usually recommend for patients, a reminder for Grace's outpatient appointment with the bone doctor, and some spare leg covers so she can shower."

Luke grunted his thanks then pushed the wheelchair into the hallway, heading to the front, where he'd parked, aware his mother trotted along behind him. "I'll go get the prescription filled and meet you both at home."

She peeled off at the front door and Luke was thankful as he repositioned the front seat so Grace could recline about halfway in the passenger seat.

When Grace moved to lever herself up, he growled, "I'll carry you, love."

She stilled. "I can get myself into the car," she muttered.

"You likely can, but right now, let me do this, alright?" He scooped her up and slid her with care, making sure not to knock the moonboot and leg. Once she was inside, he reached over, tugging the seatbelt across her, and clicking it into place.

He heard her audible sigh and glanced at her face, but she closed her eyes and settled back against the seat. After closing the door, he scooted the chair back inside quickly before returning to climb into the car and fired the ignition. "Let's go home, love," he murmured.

"Yes, please," Grace replied.

NINETEEN

Grace couldn't explain easily why she was so happy to see Luke's house again. It might be because of the peaceful scenery. The greenery certainly was lovely, and the breeze, the gentle jangle of windchimes, and the chirrup of birds was stress-relieving.

The bustle of the hospital wasn't her idea of an entertaining location either. The people coming and going and the constant waking and interruptions to take her temperature and see what her level of consciousness was had irritated her.

Some of the comfort she drew from the location could be because she felt she could relax her guard; something she'd rarely been able to do as an adult.

Maybe it was because everything about the place reminded her of Luke.

That's the key, isn't it? Luke.

She bit her lip and glanced at the front garden as he drove smoothly into the garage. "Wait and I'll come around and help you," he said, and while she wanted to tell him she could do it herself, the moonboot and crutches would make climbing out more difficult. So she simply nodded and gave in to what he suggested.

When he opened the door, he reached for her, changing her position after she loosened her seatbelt.

With her legs levered out of the car, he passed her the crutches he'd slid into the back seat. "I could carry you," he said.

"I know, but I need to do this for myself," she told him. She pushed up, leaning on the car door as she slid the crutches into her armpits and sighed. "I remember now why I hated these so much," she mused.

"I've never broken a leg, so I wouldn't know."

She stared at him. "Really? I thought most kids do."

"I don't know too many weres who've had breaks. I guess we tend to bounce better than most." He grinned at her, and she couldn't help but return the smile.

"Well, I guess since I'm not going anywhere—" And wasn't that ironic, because it's what she'd been angry about before the accident. "—you can tell me about your childhood."

"I hardly remember it, really. Weres grow at a human rate until puberty, then we slow down. You noted how young my mother looks? She's a hundred and twenty, and that's very young to be a widow in our world. Hell, I'm in my sixties and not even married. Paula is seventy next year, and that's about the average for a commitment."

Her jaw dropped. "What?"

"Like I said, we grow slowly after puberty. It's not uncommon for our kind to live into their sixth century, and things have improved remarkably in the last sixty or seventy years. I've heard of some in their seventh and eighth century."

She considered his words. "So tell me, if I mate with you—" And at that his eyes gleamed. "—will my live elongate like that too?"

"Yes, it will, love. But there's a lot of commitment in mating. For our pack, it's like marrying, and in fact, most of us marry as part of the official mating rites. Yes, there's the sexual aspect—" He stared at her as she waited. "You weren't expecting that?"

"Uh, no. I was..." Grace sighed. "I think I need a coffee and to sit down. Let's go through to the back verandah, then you can tell me what I need to know."

LUKE HAD JUST SETTLED Grace into a comfortable seat, her leg resting on another chair, and he'd made it to the kitchen to make coffee when his phone buzzed.

He picked up. "Luke Jones."

"Luke, it's David Tudor. I wanted to update you as to our ETA. We are due in Brisbane tomorrow night, coming from New York." He rattled off a flight number, and Luke reached out to grab a notepad and pen he kept on the bench and noted it. "Padraic will be in today, or more likely tonight, your time. He's flying in on a private jet."

Luke raised an eyebrow. He'd already assumed the man was loaded, but a private jet was another thing entirely. "We've had a problem with attempts to contact Grace. They're using mirrors to attempt a portal—"

"Damn," David muttered. "You have a witch to hand? I'll have Celina of the House al bin Habbad contact you, she's the master's life mate. She'll have more specific information regarding how to deal with this matter as she's a powerful witch in her own right. After the attack of Padraic's wife... She can explain what you need to know. Anyway, we're leaving soon, and we'll be in touch when we arrive."

"Thank you, David. Let me know when you arrive and what you require."

"Thank you. We'll be staying with the Concarron House in Brisbane, so we'll be nearby, I think."

With the business completed, they ended the call, and Luke frowned at the device in his hand. He knew the structure of the houses quite well, having worked with them in the past. "This is much deeper than any of use expected," he murmured.

The phone buzzed again, another international number flashing on the screen.

"Luke Jones speaking."

"Celina of House al bin Habbad. David contacted me and asked if I could assist with the situation you're facing?"

Luke blinked. "Thank you, yes. So far we've started to use a protection amulet, and our local witch is going to charge it up later today. Personalise it, so it's going to give maximum protection. And my house is heavily warded."

"That's a start," she said. "But I would suggest covers on any reflective surface, mirrors, curtains over the windows, and so on. We're dealing with an exceptionally powerful entity. The demon Marrer was partner to Ba'al Berith and has begun creating an army to overthrow Berith."

"A demonic war?" Luke wasn't up on the vagaries of spirits and fallen angels, but even he could understand this meant great danger.

"Only if we can't head it off at the pass. Padraic and Berith are working together to destroy her movement, but we believe that Grace is somehow a key in this whole mess."

Grace? How could she possibly fit in? "I don't understand, what part does Grace have to play?"

"I don't have that information. My task is merely to offer your witch some practical guidance and tips. Give her my number and explain if she needs more, she can contact me. Padraic will have any information concerning your Grace."

It wasn't nearly enough, but one didn't press the life partner of a master, so he merely thanked her for the assistance and hung up.

The kettle had boiled during the calls, so he re-boiled, taking his time considering the little nuggets of information he'd gleaned. Once the coffees were made, he headed outside with them. Settling opposite Grace, he took a moment to study her face. What could it be that was hidden behind the hex? What secrets were in her past that even she didn't know?

"David Tudor rang while I was inside."

She quirked an eyebrow.

"He's on the way, and will be here tomorrow evening. Padraic O'Shaunessy is also on his way. But I've learned a little more, Grace. It's not pretty."

"What is it?" Her brows drew together.

"Apparently, somehow, you're pivotal to a brewing demonic war. Celina, the witch life partner of Javed, said Padraic knows more, but Marrer, who is partner to Ba'al Berith, is behind it. We'll also need Thea to make sure your amulet is charged and the magic personalised, which we already knew was important."

"What else?"

"I'm going to go around, closing curtains and covering mirrors. They, whoever it is, can use portals, so we need to protect you."

"Every mirror?" Grace asked.

He nodded. "Every mirror needs to be covered. And every curtain closed too."

She stared at him. "How am I supposed to do my hair?" Then she laughed, a discordant sound. "I guess I need to suck it up, right?"

"I'm sorry, Grace. We don't have any option right now."

"No, I guess not. What else?"

"Padraic O'Shaunessy will be here tonight. He's coming in on a private jet, and he has more details about the magic, and personalities. I don't have any more than that."

Her nod was slow, and it hurt him to see that she looked tired and in pain.

"Do you need a rest?" he asked.

She sighed. "Yeah, I think I do."

"Come on then. Let's get you settled in our bed," Luke said.

She rose and began hobbling along slowly. "In *our* bed?" she questioned.

"Our bed," he reinforced. "I'm sleeping where you are, and my bed is bigger and more comfortable."

She nodded. "Sure. Whatever."

CHAPTER

TWENTY

Grace woke to the throb of her leg and a warm body nestled beside her. A glance at the clock told her three hours had passed since she'd laid down. The need to use the facilities also nudged her consciousness.

She started to slide across to the edge of the bed. The weight of the moonboot was really uncomfortable, but she guessed she'd get used to it. The paperwork she'd been given, and that Luke's mother had delivered before she'd laid down, told her when she could remove it. In her case, they suggested only for showering, and she did wonder how that would proceed. The last time she'd broken her leg, she'd had a cast, like most other kids did, so this was new territory.

"What's wrong?" Luke asked, his voice groggy.

"I need the bathroom," she muttered. If he was going to ask every time she went, it was going to get old really fast.

"Do you need anything?"

"No. But I think I should get up. If I go back to sleep, I probably won't sleep tonight," she said, grabbing her crutches and hobbling across the room. Her hand was on the doorknob when she glanced over her shoulder. "The mirror in here is covered?"

"Yeah," he said, rising. "I'll go put the kettle on for a coffee, then I probably should feed you. Mum brought groceries she thought would be best—yoghurt, fruits, and things like that. What would you like?"

Her stomach gurgled. "Yoghurt sounds like a good start," she said before entering the bathroom and shutting the door between them. It wasn't that she didn't appreciate everything he was doing, but his hovering was strange. No one had ever done that before.

"It's going to take a while," she told herself as she settled to attend to nature's demands.

When she'd finished in the bathroom she hurried—as much as she could with crutches and a moonboot—to the kitchen. He'd pulled out a stool for her at the bar, coffee and yoghurt waiting.

Luke smiled. "I'm just going to cut some strawberries and add blueberries before you dig in." He looked comfortable in the kitchen.

"You did this as a kid much?"

"Mum couldn't cook even a boiled egg when she met Dad. She didn't learn much from him in their years together. Hell, even now, anything more taxing than a grilled sandwich is beyond her." He laughed, but it was good-natured. "He taught Paula and I and had just started with the littles when he died."

"How did that happen, Luke?"

He stopped his motion and his shoulders slumped. "I... There was a meeting, it was... I was engaged as a youngster. Everyone told me not to, but I knew better, as the young do. She wasn't my mate, but I was sure that would rectify itself. She was from the other faction, those that broke away, and I wanted to marry her. We were engaged in the negotiations for the mate agreements."

"What's that?" she asked.

"Mate agreements? We don't use them much anymore because most marry their mates, so... Anyway, there were factions in our pack, those who weren't happy with Nate's dad as alpha. Things were tetchy even though we were going to marry, so Nate's dad suggested we have agreements, a bit like a prenuptial contract. It states what rights and responsibilities we agree to, division of assets in case of a breakdown, things like that." He shrugged, looking down at the cutting board and knife in his hands.

She wondered if he was replaying that day in his mind.

"Dad was adamant that since we were from differing sides of the clan, we needed to protect what we had. On that day there was an argument that got heated. He had a blocked artery none of us knew about. There's very little health-wise that can keep a were down, but it seems a blocked artery is one of the few. He had a heart attack when the meeting and agreement broke down."

"You blame yourself?" she asked, surprised that he'd take on the blame.

"Somewhat," he answered, looking—for the first time—vulnerable. "He told me that the relationship wasn't what I thought, but he'd back me if I really wanted it." Luke sliced the strawberries in silence, and she didn't say anything, aware he needed a moment. Sliding the fruit into a bowl, he passed her a spoon before sprinkling on the blueberries.

She reached out, touched his hand. "I doubt he'd blame you. And a blocked artery is something that will eventually make itself know, right?"

He smiled. "Dad was good-natured. He wanted the best for the pack. He was one of the ones that agreed to the split of the clans, because he felt that unhappy members would cause greater issues in the long-term."

"And he cooked?"

"Yeah." Now his smile was wide. "He always said that in a household someone had to know how not to burn water. I miss him, Grace. I wish you could have met him. He was a good man, and the kind of role model most weres need."

"Sounds like you were close."

He nodded. "Yeah. We really were. There was nothing better than a Saturday afternoon trip to the river or beach to catch fish. Then we'd bring them home, cook them up, and have a fish and chip feast."

"Feast?"

"Chips by the mile." He turned his head to the side. "I think, once you're better and we get this mess sorted, we should have a family night again. A fish and chip feast."

A sound echoed, and they both turned. "A fish and chip feast?" Paula squeaked. "Gods, we haven't done that in nearly twenty years!" She wandered into the room. "Sorry to barge in, but Mum said that with Grace's accident, you might need help."

She dropped her bag on the counter and pecked her brother on the cheek while Grace watched, wishing for the first time in a long while that she'd had that kind of relationship with someone. Anyone.

CHAPTER

TWENTY-ONE

The phone beeped again, and he reached for it, cursing. "Luke Jones."

"Mr Jones, this is Padraic O'Shaunessy. I've arrived in Brisbane and was wondering if there was some way we could meet tonight?"

He glanced at the clock. Seven-thirty. "I'm sorry, Mr O'Shaunessy. By the time I get in to Brisbane itself it'll be close to nine PM, and I'm not comfortable leaving Grace alone at that time of night. I could meet you in the morning though, if that's suitable?"

He heard movements over the phone. "Would it be possible for me to come to you? I have someone who can drive me, as I don't know the city very well at all."

Luke thought that wise, as Brisbane traffic and roads had become notorious over the years. With a mixture of congestion, constantly changing one-way traffic, and the GPS feeds being regularly out-of-date, reliance on apps and devices was dicey.

"Yeah, that probably would be better," Luke said, "then Grace can attend."

"Yes, I heard about your difficulties with portals. My wife, Fenella, is travelling with me, and I feel she may be able to shed light on certain aspects of Grace's issues."

Luke frowned but nodded. "Of course. I'll have Thea, a witch, meet you at the entrance to the property. We've had the wards upgraded so only specific people can enter the property until the danger is passed."

"Yes, I can understand that. It may be wise if she remains for the meeting too then. I may have another friend pop in. Now, if you could send me the address and time that suits best, I'll leave you to it."

"I'll text you the information, as there's a few tricks to finding the entrance," he said.

Once the call disconnected, he stirred the sauce he was making for the Chicken Veronique he'd put together. He wasn't trying to show off for Grace, he told himself, but she was clearly used to a higher level of food preparation and choices. Then he quickly tapped out the instructions for Padraic.

The clopping sound of Grace entering the kitchen surprised him. "Veronique?" she questioned, and he nodded. "It's one of my favourite dishes. Tasty and fairly simple, except the reduction. That can cause newer cooks some concern."

He felt her move beside him, and she investigated the reduction. "Nice," she said.

"I thought we'd eat at the inside table tonight, so I can close the door and curtains." Then he cursed silently as her grin melted away.

"Yeah, makes sense."

If he wasn't stuck at the kitchen dealing with the sauce, he'd have dragged her into his arms, hoping to dispel the concern he read on her face and the slump of her shoulders.

Grace settled on a stool and watched him. "What are you using as a side?"

"Duchesse potatoes, some steamed broccoli and carrot sticks."

"Simple is always better, but did you really make duchesse potatoes?"

He nodded. "Yep. And if I say so myself, they look pretty good. Just slightly caramelised on top, and creamy in the centre."

"Where were you when I was looking for an offsider?" she muttered.

"Setting up my private investigation company or busy with cases," he answered, trying to lighten the mood again.

"Why did you get into that field?"

"It was an accident initially. With the fracturing of the pack, it was necessary to ask questions, to find out who was on what side. It wasn't a friendly split, and there were members of the pack who were using the situation for their own personal gain. That's when I met my business partners. They were ex-police at a loose end, when being a policeman wasn't cool. They showed me the ropes, and I was a fast learner and discovered this was what I wanted to do. They front the business mostly, looking like the elder statesmen I guess, and I'm the young pup, or at least that's most humans' understanding. We don't bother to correct them. I'm not necessarily business-minded, although it's my plan to open an office near to here. The new assistant I've hired, who's starting next week, is also a local and a were."

"But your partners, obviously, are human, right?"

He grabbed cutlery from the drawer. "Would you be able to set the table?"

Taking the silverware, she hobbled to the table, and placed out mats then placed forks, knives, and spoons. "Glasses?"

He nodded. "No wine tonight—if you're off, then so am I." She opened her mouth, he assumed to protest. "No, that's how we roll, love. I will support you."

"Okay, then what would you prefer?"

"We could have cola?" he answered, so Grace grabbed tall glass tumblers for the table.

"You might need to bring the bottle," she grouched, and he smiled.

"Sure," he responded. "I will say though, that according to the literature you'll likely have another six weeks of this, so I hope you're not a grumpy hop-along."

She poked out her tongue.

"I might just bite it," he said, his voice dark and sultry.

Heat coiled inside Grace. "Don't do that unless we're able to do something about it."

"Well, I was doing some reading, and in a week or two, when you're up to it…"

He waggled his eyebrows, and she laughed, delighted in his playfulness. She'd never had any real experience of that, her few interactions with men having been shallow. An opportunity to scratch the sexual itch and no real commitment. With Luke it felt different, like she really wanted more.

The only fly in the plan was whoever this Marrer was and why she wanted Grace. She shook it off, physically and mentally. This wasn't the time to engage in question. Tonight it was just herself and Luke, and she'd make the most of the time they had together. And if by some stroke of luck, there was a forever, she wasn't going to waste their together time with doubts and fears that were beyond her current understanding.

"Feed me, man. I want a taste of that Veronique," Grace called out.

He controlled his laughter. "It's coming, you demanding woman."

She laughed and settled at the table, a feeling of well-being building inside herself.

"You don't do that enough," he said, advancing with the pan and spooning out the chicken and grape and cream sauce.

Glancing up at Luke, Grace frowned. "What?"

"Laugh." He returned the pan to the stove then came back with the vegetables on a platter. "Help yourself."

She bit her lip. "Maybe I haven't had much opportunity before now," she answered, taking the tongs to scoop up the colourful offerings.

~

MORNING CAME ALL TOO SOON, and Luke lay still, holding Grace in his arms. *I could certainly get used to this.*

The sound of birdsong wafted into the house. He had pulled the curtains closed, but he'd left the windows open. Security, given the depth of his wards, wasn't an issue, and it was just another reason why living outside of the growing town suited his needs.

Being one with nature was a balm to him. The wolf inside agreed sleepily. The warmth of Grace—not just any body—was a calming influence.

She turned with a groan, and he held her tighter, so she wouldn't hurt herself. He knew the knot on her head was still tender, and her leg was likely paining. He glanced at his bedside table, pleased he'd remembered the vial of her painkillers. When she woke, he'd offer her one, aware she was hoping to get by on as little as possible.

His clock indicated it was only seven in the morning, so he kept still, hoping she'd rest a while longer yet. He had an online appointment at one with another case, unable to escape his work completely while he had Grace around. He'd also need to check in with his partners later today and update them, and he hoped to arrange the lease for the building he'd inspected only a week before. Thankfully, a lot of the basic fit-out could be overseen by Eliza once she started working for him.

His phone buzzed, and he cursed silently. "Hello?"

"Padraic O'Shaunessy here. What time do you want to meet?"

He bit back an oath because he'd hoped for longer, but Grace was stirring. "How about nine? That will give us time to get Grace upright, and for her pain relievers to kick in."

"Pain relievers? Has she been injured?"

He sighed. "She broke her leg, falling down my back steps. She's fine, and the doctor said she'd heal quickly."

"Ah, all good then. I'll be there at nine." The man rang off.

"Who was that?" Grace asked, her voice groggy.

"O'Shaunessy. He'll be here by nine." Reaching for the vial, he rolled out a tablet. "Take this. There's water on your bedside table."

She took it, swallowed, and lay still. "It hurts," she told him.

Luke rolled over so he could see her face. The lines around her lips were pinched and white, and he ran a tender finger over her forehead. "I'm sorry it hurts, love. I'd rather you never felt anything like this ever again."

"Me too," she muttered, inhaling and exhaling, which further betrayed her discomfort.

"Give it a minute for the pill to kick in, then I'll help you..."

"I can go to the toilet by myself," she said with a sigh. "But you could grab me another dress, like the blue one you brought to the hospital for me."

Luke thanked his lucky stars that his sister had left a range of easy-wear dresses behind. He rose from the bed. "I'll get one and your underwear."

"Great," she answered, her eyes hidden by the arm she'd thrown over them.

Once he'd grabbed what she wanted and delivered it to the bedroom, he headed to the kitchen. As he made coffees and spooned yoghurt and fruit into a bowl for Grace, he dialled Thea and explained the situation to her. Grace hobbled into the room, took a seat at the bench, and watched him in silence. It was companionable, as if they'd already formed a routine that worked for them.

Settling beside her, he gripped his coffee. "You're not having breakfast with me?" she asked.

He shook his head. "Not now. I prefer to eat later, but the tablets require you to eat within thirty minutes." He sipped his drink, letting the bitterness wake him. "I have some meetings this afternoon, love. On the computer. I'll set up at the dining room table, if that suits for you. You could watch television, read, or even have a snooze."

"This is the laziest I've been in my whole life," she told him. "I'm used to working, writing lists or ordering or cooking. I'm not sure I won't go stir-crazy soon."

He considered her words. "I don't suppose you'd like to assist with an office fit-out, would you?"

She blinked. "A what?"

"The new office needs furniture, and I'm terrible at choosing colours. Are you any good at it?"

"I... Yeah, I think so."

The seed of excitement unfurled. "Then maybe you could help me pick the furniture. I need two to three working offices, a reception area, and a pool office area."

"Pool office area?"

He grinned. "It's where the assistants sit. With printers, desks, and filing cabinets."

"I don't know," she said, doubt creeping into her voice.

"I can help you, but it would keep you busy, but only if you're up to it."

Grace appeared to consider his words before she nodded. "Sure, why not? And if you don't like the colours I choose, then you could sack me."

He laughed. "I'm not sure I can sack someone who isn't an employee, but sure."

GRACE SETTLED into the lounge chair, waiting for this Padraic O'Shaunessy to arrive. She didn't know what it was that had butterflies filling her stomach at the thought of the man, but she did.

Luke was making a pot of coffee, and he laid out cups, sugar, and spoons. She had the impression he was as unsettled about the looming meeting as she was. *He's just in a better position to handle it. He can get up and move around, while I'm a beached whale.*

As each moment passed, she became more concerned. What if this man said she was a demon? An evil one. What if this Marrer was her parent?

Or even worse, what if I'm not and they have some reason to want to kill me, she asked herself. Not that she said the words aloud. *Words have power,* she told herself. *Never give someone that kind of ability to control you.*

The pep talk didn't work though, as the butterflies became an angry swarm of bees.

By the time the sound of the car in the drive heralded their arrival, she was terrified there was another darker motive as to why they needed to see her.

Nausea assailed as the front door opened, and she was wholly unprepared for the two people who followed Luke into the house.

Mr O'Shaunessy was a tall man with piercing green eyes and red hair, dressed in jeans with a gold buckle and leather boots. He was lean, but there was an air of strength about him, and he was joined by a woman with flaming red hair. She was tall with a spare frame and violet eyes that seemed otherworldly.

"Miss Cranston, I'm Padraic, and this is my wife, Fenella," he said to Grace. "I've come on a mission from... an associate. He sent me looking for the child of a friend, a girl, who went missing many years ago. He'd exhausted all his avenues and they... he asked me to assist."

She felt faint, were they talking about her? "Why would anyone be looking for a girl child?"

"Because they were taken as a way of controlling those they considered lesser than them." Padraic spoke quietly, coming to crouch before her.

Luke moved in, taking the seat beside her. "How? She was found near the motorway. Injured and alone with no memory."

"Ah, that is Marrer's way. She's a destroyer, and a young child would be easy, she may think. Tell me, Miss Cranston, you have no memory, yet there is the shadow of something hidden."

She frowned. "I'm not sure I know what you mean?"

"Have you felt the presence of someone watching you, but no one is there? Or a cold shiver in the middle of a hot room?" O'Shaunessy asked.

She scoffed, "Everyone feels that."

"Indeed, maybe and maybe not," Padraic replied.

"Padraic, don't be so cloak-and-dagger," Fenella said with a laugh. "My husband has spent too long hiding what he is and what he knows. It's the leprechaun way, but I'm not tied to that thankfully." She smiled. "Mind if I sit?"

Luke indicated they should find seats, and the couple settled themselves on the lounge chairs. "So, it seems you've had experience of demons using portal?" Luke asked.

Fenella shivered, and Padraic glowered. "Oh yes, we do at that. Have they attempted it with you?"

Grace licked her lips. "Mirrors and things like that. We have to keep the curtains closed, and Luke has covered all the mirrors."

"So Marrer has bounced back in the last two years, since we gave her a belting," Padraic explained. "When she took Fenella, my associate..."

"Oh, for feck's sake, Padraic, tell them who," Fenella rasped.

Padraic sighed. "Ba'al Berith had an inside connection. He was instrumental in getting Fenella back, but she was severely injured. It was her demon blood that kept her alive during her captivity."

Grace was stunned. He was working with a demon? Fenella was a half-demon? "I..." She shook her head. "I don't understand why they'd be coming for me though."

"Berith had a lesser demon, Vinta, who served him. Vinta had a daughter, my dear. I think... We think that could be you." Padraic's words were like a peal of bells.

In her head a cloud formed.

Dark.

Overwhelming.

It sucked the oxygen from her lungs, and the dark grey clouded across her eyes. She couldn't fight it, and when it descended, consciousness fled.

CHAPTER

TWENTY-TWO

Luke caught Grace as her eyes rolled back and she slumped. "What the fuck?" he muttered, pulling her against his body.

Fenella glanced at Padraic who frowned. "Is she alright?"

Luke seethed. "She was only released from the hospital yesterday. What the hell were you thinking?" Fury was building inside him. They came here, and without asking or thinking, dumped information that overloaded her system. He held her close, thankful that she was breathing, and the colour which had fled her cheeks—not that there'd been much—was returning.

Fenella sighed. "Apologies. He forgets sometimes that we aren't always as strong as he is."

Padraic muttered, "It wasn't my intention. But even so..."

Thea, who'd been skulking by the door, entered the room. "That's one way to find out. Any memory she has is buried under so many levels of hexes that anything that might jog her will physically affect her. We need more information before we can break through the safeguards put in place without causing further harm. I'm not sure she can psychically take a lot more of these stress events, so trial and error isn't an option." She spoke with a crispness that Luke was sure betrayed her frustration too.

"What do you mean by that?" Padraic demanded.

Thea sighed and squatted, checking Grace's pulse. "It's definitely faster, and see how her nerves are jumping? The body has a response to stresses, right? The stronger the reaction, the longer it takes for the body to recover. Each occasion becomes more overwhelming to the body. She's been living on nerves for years, and I'm guessing she's started to release some of the strong bindings on her emotions, so she's more at risk, hence the faint. What we need to do is find what the trigger is, and I'm guessing memory. I don't have anything concrete yet, but I'm going to contact Celina tonight." Thea grimaced in Luke's direction. "I didn't want to say anything just yet, but we're working on a plan. For now, we need to keep her safe and calm, otherwise she might not survive the fight against those blocks on her mind."

"That's not an option," growled Luke. "She will survive. Nothing else is an option."

His wolf was now on high alert too, sensing the emotions of the two before him. Fenella was horrified, while Padraic was clearly infuriated, if the screwed-up face and tension were indicators.

"Then how am I supposed to get her to Berith?" Padraic demanded.

Thea speared Padraic with a sharp glance. "At this time. I highly recommend you do not attempt that. Nor should you introduce Vinta, or whatever his name is. She needs to regroup her defences first. And we need David and those he's bringing with him."

"Who's he bringing?" Luke demanded.

Thea shook her head. "Witches of immense power. But our plan will take time. Maybe up to a week, and keeping her safe will be difficult."

Luke snarled. "How do I know we actually have that long?"

Thea rubbed her hand over her brow. "Realistically, we don't know that for sure. If they find her and make a grab, she's psychically at risk. Her response tells me that the glimpses in the mirror have been weakening the blocks, but the hexes are no doubt an extra precaution. A whammy to stop her…" Thea appeared to be hunting for the right word. "…exploration. If anything, I think we need to know why she was left in that location and the reason for the hexes, because that's what is holding her back."

"Berith told me that while Vinta is a lesser demon, it's what he guards that opens her to risk. He's been one of Berith's supporters for millennia. Never on the front line, but there, rounding up support when Marrer started to move against him." Padraic sighed and slouched back in the seat.

Luke growled. "So, we need to find out how she got there, and who transported her."

"Except, it's not really that simple, is it?" Fenella said.

"Depends. I've put a call in to the child safety department to see if they have detailed records. When I asked Grace, she said she didn't really have a lot of information about where she was found." Luke pondered her face, noting that she was starting to come around.

"Where… What happened?" she whispered, lifting a hand to swipe across her face.

"You collapsed. I caught you," he muttered.

"That seems to be the story of my life these days," she said. "And for the record, I'm not a fainting goat."

He smiled at the put-out tone of her words. "Never thought you were," he said.

GRACE SAT UP SLOWLY, very aware that the other three were watching her and Luke interact.

"Sorry about that," she muttered as Luke offered her a glass of water to sip.

"We're so very sorry," Fenella said, a lilt in her voice betraying her Irish heritage.

"Aye," the man, Padraic, offered.

Thea, who she'd met before, scooted forward. "I need to charge your amulet. Will you pass it over?"

Grace's hand shook as she raised it. There was something about it, the sense of security, she guessed, that made her feel uncomfortable handing it over. A glance to Luke reassured her though, as his nod indicated that this was something she should comply with. She handed over the amulet, though not happily.

Thea gripped it tight. "I'll be as quick as I can."

She may believe that, but Grace had concerns given what she'd seen in the mirror chilled her to the core. "How soon...?"

"Give me a day or two," Thea answered. "I'll cleanse it then charge it just for you. Then each month, I can boost it, so you're safe."

Grace gripped Luke's hand. "Okay," she whispered. "I just want..." She licked her lips. "I want to be me again. I hate being scared and hiding. I've always been in control, but now, I feel like I've lost part of me." It felt like her entire being was cracked, dented. Somehow, within a matter of days, she'd lost her identity. An identity she'd cobbled together after losing everything as a child.

Luke squeezed her fingers gently. "And you will be again soon. David Tudor is going to land tonight, and we can arrange a meeting."

She nodded, pushing down on her fears, because what else was there for her to do?

Sitting up, she excused herself to use the bathroom, aware she was clomping down the hall, with boot and crutches, then splashed her face, because she needed the moment to regroup. The shroud over the mirror when she looked up from the vanity unit reminded her that right now she had little to no control over what happened.

Leaving the bathroom, Grace was startled to hear a knock on the bedroom door. "Come in" she called, and Fenella entered the room.

"I hope I'm not intruding, but I hoped to have a private word with you," the Irish woman said.

"Uh, sure," muttered Grace. After all, what else could there be?

Maybe she had another head stump hidden on her back somewhere, or an uncle that was an evil magician...

"I know this all seems too much, Grace. But it does get better." The woman reached out, taking her hand and leading her to the bed, where they both sat, Grace with her leg stuck out and crutches resting on her lap. "Learning about who you are, and the secret of our reality, is hard. I'm a half-demon too, and Padraic found me when I was at my lowest. I'd lost everything my family had amassed over centuries."

Grace gawped at the woman. "How?"

Fenella coughed and laughed at the same time. "It wasn't anything I did. It was too little money, too much to do, and one young girl who couldn't save a farm alone. I'd sold it to Padraic, because he'd had an affiliation to the land. It was... I didn't know any of this at the time, but like you, I was in danger. One morning I was nearly lost to the call of the wee people, and he saved me. Yes, there's danger, but there's also a greater and more meaningful reward, Grace."

"Why are you telling me this?" Grace asked.

Fenella laughed. "Our stories are similar but different. We've both lost a lot, but we've gained a lot too. There is danger, and I won't lie to you. It hovers like a dark cloud, but... Feck me," she muttered. "I'm not good with words like Padraic, but there's a lot to gain. A life. A family, and a connection to something greater. For us, it was saving the land so evil couldn't control the portal to the veil. I don't know what your future holds, but there is some plan. As Padraic says, 'Danu plans what Danu needs.'"

"Danu?"

"Aye, she's a goddess, and Padraic says she's a right bitch. And sure, there's lots of demons to meet, not discounting Berith, who's the underworld librarian, but for all he's a demon, he is fair. He wants to neutralise Marrer because she'd take over the world."

Grace blinked at the woman. "Take over the world?"

"Aye, chaos is her aim. She can't be allowed to win, so we—those like you and I—we have a calling. Tasks we must perform to ensure she can't win. For now, I'm not allowed to say more, but when the time is right, and you need more information, you can ask me. We're all in this together. The leprechauns, the weres, the vampires, and the demons. We're all chess pieces on a board with a part to play." Fenella rose. "We should join the others, before your were gets impatient and comes to stop me talking."

Grace laughed. "I don't know that he's my were." It felt strangely comforting though to hear her say the words. It was like they held a power which was banked.

Fenella smiled. "Aye, just like me. I denied I could be with Padraic for a good while. After all, what could a braw man like him want with a scrawny, dumb, and uneducated girl like me? Turns out, he needed the love I carry for him, just as much as I needed him."

Grace considered her words. "Braw?"

Fenella waggled her brow. "Strong and well-built."

"Ah." Grace nodded. "I see. Uh…"

Fenella laughed. "It's okay, because we have the men who complete us. He's already in love with you as you are with him. He treats you like a princess, and you're trying hard to be strong." Leaning in, Fenella's words deepened. "Let him be there for you." Then she patted Grace's hand. "It'll be fine once the rest get here."

They rose and moved to the door, Grace shadowing Fenella as she considered the words of advice, thankful to know the woman had trod a similar path before. Maybe she could ask her questions.

"Fenella?" Grace said, and the woman turned. "Thank you."

"Aye," she answered. "You've only to ask, and I'll be there."

CHAPTER

TWENTY-THREE

L uke didn't know what Fenella had said to Grace, but when she returned, he could discern a lightening of the tension surrounding her—as if she knew something that bolstered her. For that, he was grateful to the woman who'd left with the Irish leprechaun.

"He's a very strong-minded man, Luke. You'll need to watch to ensure you and Grace aren't railroaded into something bigger than any of us understand," Thea warned.

Luke grunted, because although clearly Padraic was old, his aura soaked with dense magic that his wolf could almost see, Luke had already sized Fenella up, and he was sure she wouldn't stand for any such coercion. "I think we'll be fine on that front. More to the point, it's any lingering danger after this passes because of association that poses a greater risk."

Thea frowned. "I'm no precognitist, but you could be right," she conceded.

"Go home, Thea. Charge the amulet, and I'll let you know when the others arrive," he muttered. Grace had settled in for a nap; the excitement had worn her out, and it worried him that her reserves had been so depleted already.

Thea left with a promise, "I'll check the wards on my way out. If they need a boost, I'll get the others to join me tomorrow."

"Thank you," he said, watching as she left through the front door.

He'd only opened the curtains once Grace had settled, but he had the distinct feeling that the sun shining in wasn't bright or friendly as he normally found it. Today it felt like there were clouds rolling in.

"I won't let them hurt her," he said to himself. But the bravado was just that. *How can I fight a danger I can't see and don't understand?*

Sliding the curtains to a close, Luke snatched up the phone as it started to trill. "Luke Jones."

"Mr Jones, our flight made excellent time and we've landed. I wonder if we could meet you both for a meeting in a few hours?" David Tudor's voice was strong, forceful, yet Luke had the impression he wasn't being railroaded.

"Mr Tudor—"

"David," the other man corrected.

"Uh, David. That would certainly be possible. However, our witch has taken Grace's amulet to charge, and as we're behind a strong ward, it would be simpler if you could come to me."

"Yes, although the meeting will need to be after dark. I am joined by several vampires who believe they may be able to assist with this matter. Including Javed, the Master of the House al bin Habbad, and his life partner, Celina. They have some insight which would be useful."

Luke frowned. A master vampire and a witch of immense power. What the fuck had he fallen into, and how the hell was he going to explain this to Nate and his mother?

"Mr Jones?"

"Luke," he muttered. "My name is Luke."

"Of course, but Luke, I need to know—"

"Yeah," he answered. "I just need to let a few people know."

"The fewer the better," David replied. "We cannot afford for Marrer to catch on yet. While she's not yet at full strength, we're going to need every trick to deal with this mess."

"Do you wish me to make contact with Padraic?"

David chuckled. "No, it's okay. I know where my wife's father is staying, and I'll be seeing him soon."

It took a moment for that to settle in. "Of course."

The call was quickly wound up, and Luke was rising when Grace came clomping down the hall. "Who was that?" she asked.

Her hair lay in soft waves around her shoulders, and he wondered if she had any idea that the tiny camisole she'd slipped over her nakedness, or the lycra shorts, covered very little? He could clearly see the outline of her rosy nipples, and they jutted through the light cotton.

She's injured, so down boy, he told his inner libido. It wasn't listening if the sudden tightening in his groin was anything to go by.

Grace cocked her head to one side. "What's wrong?"

"Nothing," he growled, frustrated with his apparent lack of control.

"Nothing, huh? I was waiting for you, Luke."

"The phone rang," he muttered.

"Whatever it was, clearly it wasn't a pleasant call," she replied with a tight smile.

"It's..."

"Nothing, yes, I get that, Luke. And if you don't want to tell me, that's okay too. Just, maybe don't bite my head off." Her lower lip wobbled, and he cursed, feeling like a grubby heel.

"No, it's not that, Grace. I mean, I just... I'm looking at you and I'm..." He sighed and shook his head. "I want you."

She looked at him, clearly bewildered by his statement. "What?"

"I want you. Sexually. And you're injured. So what does that make me?"

Her glance was startled. "You want me?" The squeak in her voice surprised him.

"Yes, love. But you're not up for that. Not yet. With your leg, I could hurt you."

She cleared her throat. "I... I guess you startled me, Luke. Or maybe surprised is a better description." She moistened her lips with the tip of her tongue, and he couldn't control the groan that rose.

"You're killing me, Grace."

She smiled; a wide 'I've got you now' grin. "Well, I can't say that I've ever driven a man wild, but it appears you're hungry for... food."

Surprise rippled through him. "Food?"

She shook her head. "Okay, as much as I'd like to partake, I agree. My leg is hurting, and I just took some pain pills. But I'm hoping that soon..."

He grunted, taking her in his arms with a gentle move. "When you're well enough, my love. Until then, I will stay by your side, make sure you are safe."

She sighed and nestled into his embrace. "Is this a 'you' or a 'were' thing? 'Cause, I have to say, what you're selling, it's powerful stuff, Luke."

"Call me..." He swallowed the word, because he knew she wasn't ready for it.

"Call you what?" she whispered against his ear.

He shuddered. "You're not ready yet, love."

"Tell me. Let me make my own decision."

"I want you to call me mate," he said and held himself still.

"I want to, but I... I'm not ready."

"I know," he growled. "But one day, you will. Until then, I'll be patient and wait for you. I'd wait forever," he promised.

"I want to believe that. I know you do, but I need time. You tell me you have your wolf who insists this is the case, but I don't." She pulled away, her gaze roaming his face. "I want to have someone love me for me. I want to be loved, but I don't yet have the surety of that. I don't make statements like that without being sure. I so want what you're offering, but I need to check first."

He nodded. Understanding that her childhood left her with

scars, he'd already concluded she'd need time to heal and to come to terms with his emotional attachment to her. "I know, and I'm waiting for you, Grace."

She tugged away. "I'd love a coffee, Luke."

"Yeah, come on and I'll get it." He shadowed her as she moved down the hall to the kitchen. "I'm kind of surprised we've had any quiet time. I half-expected Mum to turn up here, or Paula."

"I think I'm going to need someone to talk to soon. I don't know a lot about…"

"About what, love?" He waited as she settled herself onto the stool.

"Weres. I mean, I don't even know that I was sure they existed." She shrugged. "I knew about the vampires, because they came out, but weres didn't have the same level of visibility."

"We prefer it that way. I guess it lets us live reasonably safe lives. Most have settled in areas outside of cities, we bought tracts of land, so we wouldn't be built-out. We need hunting grounds, and we couldn't really live in cities easily if there weren't natural zones. Not that the local councils or state governments give a shit."

She reached out a hand as he slid the coffee he'd made across the benchtop. "What do you mean?"

"There are a number of weres in government, but they don't seem to be concerned about the needs of their kind. They ignore the representations the clans have made."

"Are any from your pack?"

He shook his head. "No. They're from the other side. Having said that, Nate is considering that he should stand. We need someone capable of arguing for our needs."

Luke made his way around the bench to the stool beside her, and she reached out and took his hand. "I…"

A bang echoed, and the house shook. "What the fuck was that?" he growled, head snapping up, eyes narrowed as the screeching of metal filled the air.

Grace dropped his hand, her face white, and her eyes wide. "Luke?"

He jumped down, flashing so fast to wolf mode that his clothing tore. He captured her gaze, shook his muzzle, then dashed away. He'd find out what that was, and he'd deal with it.

GRACE'S MOUTH DROPPED OPEN, watching the magical change from man to wolf. One second, he'd stood beside her as a man, then it was a jet-black wolf with silver sprinkles through the pelt.

His eyes hadn't changed though, the same grey-blue, and it had been impossible to misunderstand the fury in his gaze. He'd shook his muzzle at her, and she knew she needed to remain where she was. Not for the first time, she cursed the broken leg, but there was nothing she'd be able to do right now. Not while she was lugging a moonboot and a pair of crutches.

He turned and leaped away, leaving her alone.

Her fingers curled into tightly clenched fists, but even as she sucked in an unsteady breath, the house shook again.

She squeezed her eyes shut. "What's going on?"

No one was there to answer her.

A howl went up from outside; a wild cry.

Another echoed, then a third and a fourth.

Snapping her eyes open, she looked out into the backyard as wolves broke cover, sprinting to the house, as if called by some supernatural being.

The house trembled, and Grace pushed herself up from the stool, a sudden urgency beating at her. "I have to get out of here," she muttered as glasses tinkled in the kitchen and the curtains started to sway.

She limped as quickly as she could, the thud of the crutches on the floors echoing as she made for the front door. The floors undulated beneath her, and her hand was on the knob of the door. It heated, and she cried out but twisted it, flinging the door open, and lunged outside.

～

THE WOLVES SURROUNDED Luke as he tried to run for the house, hearing the sounds of rending wood and steel, the smashing of glass. "Let me go!" he screamed as his chest burned. "She's still in there!"

Panic—a suffocating bubble in his chest—stole his ability to breathe.

"Grace!" He howled as the wolves circled him, holding him back. Keeping him away.

He fought, but there were too many and he couldn't break through the barrier.

One wolf stepped back. Luke saw the move, tried to run in that direction, his brain telling him this was his only chance to get to her.

It was the biggest of the lot, and he knew before it took human shape that it was his friend Nate. "It's not safe," Nate called as he grabbed Luke in a bear hug.

"I don't care! She's still in there!" Luke's bellow was nearly lost under the final rumble as walls collapsed and the roof caved. "I have to get to her!" Nothing else was an option, but his mind was splintering. How could she possibly survive what was swiftly becoming an inferno? Flames leaping into the sky while black, billowing clouds covered the sun.

Nate didn't loosen his grip, and Luke's arms and legs kept moving, while sheer terror whipped around him, his heart beating hard. Grey spots appeared in his eyes, obscuring his vision.

"Grace! I can't lose her. She's my mate!" His inner wolf howled too, demanding he try harder, that he should transform once more.

A scream went up, and he turned...

Wavering in the distance was a figure, gripping crutches and moving slowly, hampered by that bloody moonboot. He stared as she came closer, her wild hair sticking out everywhere. Grace had survived!

"Grace," he called. He'd never seen a more beautiful sight, but tears were streaking her cheeks. She needed him, and he wouldn't let her down!

Nate's fingers, the ones digging into the flesh of his arms, were nothing now, a puny impediment that Luke swatted away before leaping over the clan members who'd been hunting in his bushlands before he'd sent out the cry for help.

Grass wavered beneath him as he rushed toward her, his wolf scenting the acrid tinge of terror on the air, but also the subtle scent of Grace.

Capturing her in his arms, he sent up a prayer of thanks to the life-giver who'd protected her. "Thank the Gods," he growled.

"What happened to the house?" she muttered against him, her arms vices that told him just how close to the edge they all were. "Luke?"

"I don't know, love. The rumbling..."

Flames leapt up from the house, and he scooped her up, dragging her as far away as he could, because the scorch of heat might hurt her. She'd survived this far; he wouldn't let anything else touch her.

They slumped to the grass, the wolves standing sentinel in the distance as cars came screaming into the yard.

He recognised Paula's and Thea's vehicles. A fire engine followed in short order, but Luke knew it was too late. He couldn't raise a care though, because in his arms was his world.

CHAPTER

TWENTY-FOUR

Grace shook, the adrenaline of escape and knowing Luke was also alive had long since left, and she huddled on the lounge in Luke's mother's house. The clothes she wore were new—again. The nightgown long and soft, not a design she'd have chosen, with lacey edging and soft ribbons. She ran her fingers along the edges. It wasn't that she didn't like anything Paula had purchased. Just that they were all high-end brands, with pretty decorations. In the past, Grace had restricted herself to utility clothing choices. This was... different.

Luke had told Paula only a list of items, but his sister had chosen things she'd have wanted but never purchased. It was as if she was channelling the life Grace could only hope for.

A tear dribbled down her cheek. "I'm not a wimp," she told herself, but the normal ferocity she'd employ was gone. Melted away like snow in summer.

Luke came toward her, as if he'd read the misery lodged inside her. "Grace?"

"I've brought so much danger with me. Your mother—"

"Knows exactly what's happening. Padraic and Fenella, along

152

with David and his entourage, will be here soon. If you want to meet with them?" He brushed her face with tender fingertips.

Grace nodded. "I have to," she said, voice hitching on the emotion.

If they could survive, then maybe there was hope that she could explore this... whatever it was between them. Heaven knew, she'd heard him say time and again that he was her mate, but as much as she wanted to accept that without question, wanted to hold onto the certainty, she needed more.

"I don't..." She shook her head, ending the question before it could be said.

"What don't you...?" He crouched down beside her.

The words tumbled forward, like a dam whose wall had broken. "You believe in me, and I don't understand why you keep protecting me, Luke. *You lost your house!*" Why would he give all that up for her? "I know you keep saying we're meant to be together, but how can you be so certain? After everything I've cost you?"

"Because you're my mate." He stared at her, and she had the impression he was trying to impress that on her at a psychic level.

Grace shook her head. "No, that's not enough for me. I don't understand, Luke. I mean, you barely know me. And the me you're seeing? It's certainly not my finest or my—"

He placed a finger against her lips. "Because I'm seeing you when you're weak and hurt. Because I see the battle you're putting up, the way you keep trying to push through. It tells me that when times are tough, you're not just going to cut and run on me. It tells me you're committed. It tells me that even though you're hurting and lost, you've got more courage than anyone else I've met."

She stared at him. "What choice do I have, Luke? This needs to end before I can even begin to sort out my emotions." The last words were growled under her breath.

"Ah, love, if only life were that simple. But for wolves, and weres, it's more than biological. It's... I guess it's finding the other half or needing an essential part of our soul, and for me—for us, my wolf and I—that's you."

"And if, that's *if*, mind you, I agree, do we have to go through all this folderol that Paula and… what's his name?"

"Nate," Luke answered with a grin. "And yes and no. He's the alpha, so usually it's a much bigger thing. And as I explained before, I think? Since the fracturing, we've formalised a lot of the processes. But there's also a private aspect for you and I. One that Nate and Paula won't need to go through." His eyes glowed.

"What?" she asked, suddenly wary and excited by equal share.

"I share my life essence with you, and you share with me." Power imbued his words, and she shook, her body instinctively reacting, nipples tightening and heat filling her belly.

She licked her lips and he watched, his gaze narrowing on her mouth. "How?"

"Through the bite, my love. We share our blood, and the essence of the were, the magic, if you will, does the rest. I haven't had personal experience with that, nor has anyone I know. I asked," he said before she could query it.

"Oh." It was layer upon layer of new experiences and knowledge. *Will I ever understand it all?* The thought shocked her for a second, then she realised it was indicative of the level of trust she felt for Luke. And the connection.

"Grace?"

"You said the others would be here soon. I need to change, I'm not meeting them in a nightgown." Yes, she avoided answering the question he didn't ask, because she needed time to think. To weigh and measure all that was happening.

A knock on the door forced Luke to stand and move away. He cracked it open, and his mother slid through and into the room. "Thea and her crew have finished, and they sent this for Grace."

In her hand was the amulet Thea had taken to charge magically.

Once again panic assailed Grace. "Did they say how they'd make sure the same thing doesn't happen here?"

Luke's mum nodded. "They said that Marrer must have used a tremendous amount of magic to push you out of the house, and she'll need time to regroup. Because of that, we have time. Thea said they'll be back tomorrow to sprinkle the grounds with imbued salt, and Luke, they'll burn sage at the house site."

Luke snarled, and guilt assailed Grace. If he hadn't tried to protect her, he wouldn't have lost everything. He must have read the negative emotion on her face, because he said, "It's not your fault, Grace."

"It is," she muttered. "All this is because of me."

LUKE STALKED INTO THE LOUNGE, giving Grace time to change and needing time to think.

"She's teetering on the edge, Luke. You'll need to watch, or she'll run."

He nodded at his mother's warning. "I know. I had Thea add a spell to the necklace so I can track her if needed, but I'm hoping David and whoever he's bringing will have more information. Padraic and Fenella will be coming too."

"So, maybe in the dining room is the best place for you to talk. Will Nate and Paula...?"

He nodded. "Yeah, I asked them to come, because if we need the pack, we'll need to gain his approval first." He ran his fingers through his hair.

"And you're only holding on by a thread, aren't you, son?"

"Mum, I'm... I don't know how to keep her safe. We don't know enough, and it's killing me." He squeezed his eyes shut.

"You're doing everything you can. Stay strong, Luca." She hugged him quickly then released as a knock heralded the first arrivals.

CHAPTER

TWENTY-FIVE

Grace moved slowly, wishing she didn't have to do this, but knowing there was no alternative.

She heard the voices and followed them into a large dining room at the far end of the house. The walls were the same peachy-cream as all the others in the house, but the tiles on the floor were covered in rich red carpeting, and the table, a long rectangle of dark wood, was flanked by matching chairs that faced an old-style fireplace. The kind you saw in history books with a high mantel and matching vases holding bouquets of fresh flowers.

Luke waited for her, his hands resting on the backs of two empty chairs. Looking around the room, she noted Padraic and Fenella, Nate—who she'd first met in the meadow—and Luke's sister Paula. Thea leaned against a wall, and four others waited, their eyes assessing her.

"Come sit, love," Luke said, "and I'll introduce you to those you don't know."

She clomped in, wishing, not for the first time, that she could be free of the moonboot and crutches. Settling in, she sighed and scanned the unknowns. The woman sitting beside Padraic was

156

clearly related to him, with the same intense green eyes and red hair. Her hand was entwined with another man beside her. He was well-groomed and dressed in what Grace guessed was a very expensive shirt and jeans, with dark hair and a keen gaze following her moves.

Grace gulped, because the last two people waiting exuded tremendous power. It licked over her, filling the air she breathed. She'd seen the man before. Javed al bin Habbad, the newest of the houses of New York's master. She might not often catch the news, but the coverage of Creedar and his attacks worldwide had dominated news for months. Grace knew that the woman beside Javed was his life partner, Celina. The witch had flame-red hair and a beauty that was almost unearthly, and she had been featured on many magazine covers.

Luke slid into the seat beside Grace. "I know who most of them are, Master Javed and Mistress Celina. The other two, I'm not..." he said.

"David Tudor, and I'm his wife, Genevieve," the woman spoke up, her voice strong with a clear American accent. "We come from the American Pack to offer support and assistance. My father, Padraic—" She indicated to the man, and Grace felt shocked because they looked near enough in age to be siblings. "—was given the task of finding you."

"By who?" she asked.

Luke's hand squeezed hers. "We can't tell you because of the hexes, love. That's what causes you to faint every time we trigger a memory."

"Oh," Grace muttered. "That seriously sucks," she said, aggrieved that knowledge clearly had to be withheld from her.

"I believe, after discussions with our librarian, that we may have found a way to circumvent that," Celina offered. "There's a ceremony we can undertake, but it's neither easy nor quick. I've discussed it with Thea, and she believes, as do I, we can amass enough power to unpick the threads, as it were, of the magic which is binding you."

"What are we waiting for then?" Grace said, and Luke squeezed her hand again.

"In your current form, we're worried you won't survive it," Thea answered. "It's never been tried on a human, and that's your current form. Vampires, weres, and even fairies as they are inherently magical, but if you're what we think you are…" And she skirted the words that might set Grace into another faint. "We can't be sure your body has the necessary protections."

"What does that mean?" Grace asked.

Luke snarled. "I can't ask that of her. She's not sure and I won't…"

Thea sighed. "We know, but it's the only way to save her, Luke. She needs the extra charge that comes from your essence. You know your wolf has told you she's your mate."

They want us to mate? Is that what… "What? You want us to exchange life essences? I don't even know if…" *But you do, don't you? You know in your heart that you belong together.*

Celina nodded, her eyes shining in the artificial light of the room. "I don't see any other way. I'm sorry. I know neither of you are ready yet. I wouldn't ask it if I thought there was another option to protect you. I do understand that you feel we're stripping you of choices, Grace. I do. *I've been there too.* Ask Javed. He saved me, but in doing so, turned me, without my free will. Sometimes though, you must take a leap of faith." She reached out. "I've no way to make you trust me, but in all things, I can honestly tell you, this is your best chance of survival."

The words fell on her, each weighty.

Which was the right thing? Walk away? Pain spiralled through her at the thought of never seeing Luke again.

Or you can mate with him.

She turned to the man beside her, so still and tense. "Luke?"

He rubbed a hand over his brow. "I'm not going to force you, Grace. Whatever we do next, it's your decision." He grimaced, and she read uncertainty in his features as he clasped his hands together. The fine tremor though betrayed his concern.

"I... Can I speak with you privately?" she asked him.

He nodded. "We need a moment." And he scraped back his chair, waiting for her to rise and slide the crutches under her arms.

Luke waited. He knew what Grace wanted and needed to know. He hated that her options were being stripped away, but if Celina was that concerned, then maybe he should encourage Grace to make the decision.

"Forcing her would not be the right move."

As usual, his wolf was right. He didn't want her to regret, at some future stage, taking the chance of something else. No matter how much that might hurt.

"What... Do you want me to mate with you?" Her question rocked him.

"I..." He stared at her. "I want you as my formal mate, but Grace, this is a lifelong commitment. It's sharing our essence and souls. It's not something we can change our mind about." He needed her to understand the gravity of her decision.

She nodded absently. "You're sure I'm your mate?"

"We both are," he confirmed, waiting and hopeful, but wary of adding pressure.

"Do you bite me, and I bite back, and it's done?" Her voice was soft.

He reached out and took her hand. "No, it's more than that. We share our bodies too, Grace. We make love, and during that time, we form a bond of power which forces the powers to rise, and my teeth will extrude." He couldn't think of a way to soften it. He'd heard tales of those who'd attempted it without the bond, and the disastrous outcome was one he'd avoid at all costs.

"What if it doesn't work?"

"It will, Grace. So long as we're both committed to each other." His gut churned at the thought that the mating might not work.

She scanned his face, her eyes wide as she bit her lip. "I want to mate with you," she whispered.

He released the pent-up breath he didn't realise he'd been holding. "Then we clear everyone out. Once we start, I want privacy for both of us."

She nodded, glancing away.

"It's not too late to change your mind," he told her.

She glanced back, and he had to swallow his next words, because there was lust and more in her gaze. "I'll... uh, do I need to...?" She waved her hand in the direction of the room beyond.

Luke shook his head. "I'll clear them out and arrange for them to come back tomorrow evening."

"Why... Oh, the vampires?" she asked, and Luke nodded. "Alright," she whispered, then turned and limped away, back up the hall.

CHAPTER

TWENTY-SIX

G race hovered in the bedroom, wondering how the hell they were going to manage with her broken leg. She snarled and hobbled to the bathroom. "At least I can look reasonable," she said, before remembering that removing the cover from the mirror wasn't an option.

The amulet she now wore as a matter of course hung around her neck, though she grasped the pendant section in her hand. It bit into the flesh of her palm, and she balanced herself against the wall, sliding the pendant back and forth around her neck and sighing as the cooling sensation covered her body once more.

Needing a moment longer, she scooped up the brush and tugged it through her hair, then a quick spritz of deodorant followed. The dress she'd chosen, a button-down shirtwaister, was loose and comfortable and hid the pretty green matching underwear. She silently thanked Paula for the foresight of purchasing matching items. At least, if her life was going to change, she wanted it to be as positive as possible. And this was certainly better than the ugly briefs and utilitarian bras she usually opted for.

Once settled on the edge of the bed, she set about releasing the straps on the boot and sliding her leg free. The soft inner lining had some light boning, so she wasn't too concerned that they'd do further damage. Or at least she hoped not.

Luke entered the room, looking about as uncertain as she was. "Grace? You're sure?"

She nodded and patted the side of the bed. "Come sit beside me."

He moved slowly. "We'll need to be careful of your leg," he muttered.

"Yes," she answered. "But I'm not made of glass." As he seated himself beside her, she asked, "Do you want this? I mean, it's all well and good to keep asking me, but you're also affected."

Heat infused the look he sent her way as he twisted beside her. "I want nothing more, Grace. I want to share your body and your life. I want to know that for as long as I walk this earth, you'll be beside me. Through good times and bad."

His words were a vow, and one she welcomed. Inside her chest, love bloomed. "Then kiss me, Luke. Show me what you want," she whispered as their mouths met.

The caress was soft, lighter than the brush of a butterfly wing. His breath slid over her lips, "I love you, Grace."

Her eyes shut as heat burst inside her. Her hands found the broadness of his shoulders and held tight as he deepened their pleasure, mouths opening so his tongue could surge deep inside, claiming and branding.

His hands circled her waist and tugged her closer while her body burned with a yearning hunger.

Once fully engulfed by him, she surrendered herself to him and the moment, raising her head, extending her neck, while he kissed his way down her jaw. His tongue tickled the sensitive spot beneath her ear, and a flash of sensation zinged through her.

"Oh Gods, Luke. I want you so much," she muttered.

"I'm all yours now. Always yours, love." The words were a sultry cadence, and her fingers left his shoulders, found the buttons on her dress. He brushed them away. "Let me," he muttered and set to work, releasing them before moving to the next fastener, and once they were finally freed, he slipped the material from her shoulders.

"You're beautiful," he said, sitting back just enough to look her over as she perched on the edge of the bed in bra and knickers.

"Perhaps, but I think you're overdressed," she said and reached for his belt buckle.

He slid her hands away. "Lie back and watch," he said.

He stood and shucked his clothes while watching her reaction. Her mouth dried when he finally pushed down his briefs so that his cock, hard and deliciously ready, sprang free.

"Like what you see?" he demanded.

"Yes, but I'd like it more if you were here, beside me," she said with a smile.

He stalked forward, muscles rippling, and her body melted further with need.

"Now you're the one who's overdressed."

She smiled. "So I am. Would you like to open your present, or shall I?"

"Just the bra first. I want to see your breasts. Those nipples are like raspberries, all hard and red. Waiting for me to feast on them." His words were carnal, and she had to squeeze her legs together, but it increased the sensations and she gasped.

"Hot and ready, are you? Waiting 'til I check? Shall I use my hand or my tongue?"

Grace gulped. "I..."

"Which would you prefer, Grace? Shall I lick you? Taste you?"

Her fingers fumbled on the catch of her bra, because he hadn't yet touched her and she was melting and so damn ready for him, his cock so close and at mouth height. She slid the straps down her arms once the catches freed and thrust the bra away before turning and capturing him with her mouth.

He hissed. "That's dangerous territory," he growled, pulling away. "Too much and we won't make it."

She snickered, "We could try again." She waggled her eyebrows.

"Nah, I'm not one to waste a good thing." He hooked his fingers into her panties, sliding them down her legs. "Look at you, lying there ready. Open your legs for me, Grace. Let me see all of you." She did, and he hissed again. "Pretty pussy," he whispered, leaning in. "Ready for me."

He climbed between her legs, his smile pure devilry. "One taste," he said. And he moved, widening her so he could bend down and slide his tongue the length of her.

The heat and erotic pleasure of his caress had her crying out his name as her fingers twisted in the material of the bed sheets, grounding her as the spiral of need wound tight. When he nudged the tiny bundle of nerves with the tip of his tongue, she swore bright lights flickered against her eyelids.

She shook and burned as he made his way up her body, finding her navel. Her abdominal muscles clenched before he continued his upward investigation. He paid careful attention to each breast, flicking their nubs before closing his mouth over one breast then the other, sucking deep as his fingers toyed between her legs.

A finger slid deep. "I can feel how close you are, Grace. I need you to come for me. Let go, my love, and feel the pleasure I wish for you."

She fought it because her brain, sluggish and drugged, told her there was more, something else she had to do.

"Luke, I want you inside me," she crooned.

"I am, sweetheart. Feel me touching you."

"More," she demanded.

"Tell me what you want then."

"I want all of you. I want your cock inside me. I need you to fill me, Luke."

"Open your eyes, my love. See me." He moved, rolling them both to their sides, then carefully positioning himself so their bodies nestled together. "Feel me as I fill you," he urged and slid hard inside.

She bowed up, sensations unlike anything she'd ever felt overwhelming her.

"Oh, Grace. Tell me now, are you ready?"

"Yes," she replied and watched as his eyes changed, the wolf and man merging, while the length of his teeth told her he was seconds away.

He laid his mouth against her neck and slowly, infinitely slowly, they pierced the flesh.

Pleasure flashed, and instinct urged her to follow his lead. Grace laid her mouth beside his throat and followed him, so she too bit deep.

Copper coated her tongue, and she lapped, needing this and more. Feeling the heat and magic of the moment, as their bodies moved, undulating faster and wilder, the release just out of reach until one last thrust came, splintering her mind.

Her fingers gripped, needing him, an anchor in the maelstrom.

Then she slumped, mouth falling away as he did the same.

His arms circled her waist, but he was still embedded inside her.

A second wave, slower and calmer than the last, washed over her, and her entire body shivered in response.

He tugged away, and she mewled. "I'm pulling up the covers, love, not leaving."

"Good, don't ever leave," she murmured sleepily and closed her eyes.

LUKE HELD HER CLOSE, the scent of sex and mating in the air. Their lovemaking had been explosive and wild, yet it soothed something inside him he'd never really acknowledged.

It was Grace. Everything was Grace. She was his light, his heart.

"You're my soul," he told her before closing his eyes and giving in to sleep.

CHAPTER

TWENTY-SEVEN

Grace's head hurt, and she didn't feel exactly one hundred percent, but at least the dull ache in her leg had stopped.

Opening her eyes, she spied Luke hovering by the bed, a frown on his face, and he was dressed in track pants and a t-shirt.

"Why are you up? We just went to sleep," she said, feeling groggy and unrefreshed. But then again, maybe that had more to do with the athleticism of last night's activities, she thought.

He smiled, but it was tight. "That was last night, nearly twelve hours or so ago, Grace."

"Oh." She tried to rise, but he pushed her back down to the mattress.

"I brought you a drink and something to eat." He perched on the side of the bed and gestured to a bag and cup on the side table. "Then the doctor wants to examine you. They're waiting outside the room."

"What? Why?"

The skin on his cheekbones turned a dull red. "We, uh... I need to make sure we didn't bump your leg or..." He shrugged.

166

"Oh." She felt the heat of his embarrassment on her own cheeks. "Okay, well, yes, I guess I should see him." Not that she wanted to, but still...

Luke rose and reached for a robe. "You may want this, love," he muttered, and she realised she was still naked from the night before even as he slid back into the bed, beside her.

"I... Give me a minute," she said. "I need the bathroom too."

She slid her leg into the waiting boot before winding the robe around herself. It felt odd to be comfortable naked when on the other side of the door someone was waiting for her.

She tottered to the bathroom, once more cursing the crutches before returning. "The doctor is..."

"My mother's doctor, and she knows what I am, and you too."

Grace looked at him. "Me?"

He smiled. "Hair growth, especially in the early days, is a common side effect for women according to Dr Hastings."

Her fingers slid to her upper lip. "What hair?"

"Your legs," he said with a tiny laugh.

Glancing down, Grace saw that the legs she'd shaved days ago were downright hairy. "Oh my God!"

He laughed. "She'll help you out there. Don't worry, it will pass," he assured her.

Grace closed her eyes and inhaled. Life had changed, the only question was, would that change help her in the next phase? Or had this all been for nothing?

Reality impinged. It wasn't for nothing, because she and Luke were now mated. In her heart, she knew that meant they were stronger and would stick it out. No matter what faced them.

"I love him," she said. Acknowledging the attachment was important, she knew.

"I love you too," he answered. "Now get back in the bed. You need to eat then rest, because Celina and the crew will be here in a few hours, and I want to know that whatever happens, you're ready for it. Because I won't let you go, Grace."

She followed his direction, sliding back under the covers.

His hand touched her face, and she cupped it, feeling his strength. "I won't let go either," she muttered. "Now, don't keep the doctor waiting."

He rose and opened the door, and the doctor stepped into the room. "You must be Grace. Don't worry, I've looked after all the kids in the family and Lillian—Luke's mother—since she came here. Now then, Luke, out you go."

Luke left the room, but not without a scowl before closing the door behind him.

"You're a were?" Grace asked.

The doctor laughed. "Yes, born and bred. Now, let's get a look at your leg and see if it's going alright, shall we?"

Grace sighed and pushed back the covers. "My legs are hairy," she wailed.

"Ah, yes. Recently mated, from human or some kind of human-based background I take it—can't ever be too sure until all the DNA is catalogued these days. Anyway, sometimes this hair growth thing can be an issue, and for women, it's more of a trauma. My suggestion? Shave today if it bothers you, then get yourself an epilator. Waxing and so on probably won't be sufficient, because in the short-term, this may well be a constant, and having to book in for treatment can be both time consuming and costly. Having said that, it does vary from person to person. Usually after the first pregnancy it settles down."

Grace blinked. "Pregnancy?"

The doctor shoved a card into her hand. "When you're ready, ring the number and make an appointment, and we can discuss all the things you want to know but don't feel comfortable asking Lillian, Paula, or even Luke." Her hands slid down Grace's leg. "You had a broken leg?"

Grace nodded as the doctor pulled a small, portable x-ray machine from her bag. It looked like a weird camera but... "Is that one that dentists use?"

The doctor nodded. "Yes, a portable system. Why?"

She shrugged. "The only time I've seen one like that is on a ship."

"Yes, they are popular there, but I keep it for working with children, particularly those in unusual fostering positions."

"Oh." Grace watched as she set to work, scanning her leg. "You don't need me to get rid of the hair?"

"No, no. It's all good."

"Hmm," and "isn't that interesting," the doctor muttered before sliding the unit back into her bag. "Well, it seems your mating has paid off in more ways than one. I can see where the break was, but you've acquired similar healing properties to most weres, in that your break has healed overnight. And that is probably more to do with the hair situation than not."

"What?" Grace didn't understand.

"I'm guessing you know a little bit about were physiology, but let me see if I can explain it briefly." She touched her nose as if considering how to explain, then held up a finger. "When a were is injured, they usually transform. It's how their body heals itself in that situation. And yes, transformational magic is involved. In your case, your body hasn't fully embraced the changes, either physiological or magical, so instead, it appears you've had a partial transition. That's the reason the hair has made an appearance." She pointed to Grace's leg. "The x-ray shows the break site is visible, but in a human, it would be the equivalent of three to four months of healing time, so it's very advanced. That means, no moonboot or crutches are needed from this point on."

Her mouth dropped open. "Really?"

"Absolutely. So you can get up and at it, but maybe show a little caution on the swinging from chandeliers until you get the hang of the change, okay?"

"And the hair?"

The doctor grinned. "As I said, a partial transformation means sprouting hair in inconvenient places. You should check underarms and other interesting spots."

Grace blushed hard.

"It happens. I would say it's human, but it's not. It's part of being a female were. And remember, make an appointment to come in and see me. Soon. We'll need to discuss prophylactics."

With a smile, the doctor slid the last of her instruments into the bag and left the room. Then Luke barged in. "Well?" he asked.

"It seems I've had a partial transformation. The leg looks like a human three to four months after a break. No moonboot or crutches. But... *hair*!" The last word emerged on a wail. "I need to shave then buy something to remove it. Can you ask Paula..."

He nodded and passed her the phone. "Send her a text and let her know what you need."

LUKE WAITED until Grace was settled in the lounge then sat beside her. "Did the doctor say anything else?"

Grace shook her head. "Not really. She checked my leg. Was there anything...?"

He wondered if she'd spoken to Grace about the possible outcome of mating sex. After all, it was when they were at their most potent. But he sure wasn't going to mention that right now, not in his mother's lounge room. It was enough that she'd been grinning ever since returning from Paula's, aware of what they'd done the night before.

"Luke dear," she now called from the kitchen. "Would you like to come make drinks? I've been helping Paula pack up her house, and I'm positively dead on my feet."

He had a sneaking suspicion his mother wanted to find out what Dr Hastings had to say on the matter of the two of them. He might wish to avoid the discussion, but he wasn't going to ignore her call, so he made his way slowly to where she waited.

Before she could leave the kitchen, he grabbed her with gentle hands. "Mum, no pumping for information. Anything Grace wants to tell you, she will. When she's ready."

She smiled and patted his cheek. "Of course, dear. No pumping today." Then she tittered and left the room.

TWENTY-EIGHT

As the night before, the twelve of them gathered in the dining room. Padraic and Fenella, David and Genevieve, along with Celina and Javed on one side, Thea and Luke's mother, Paula and Nate, Luke and Grace on the other side.

"We need to clear everything off the table and everything off the walls," Celina instructed. "The carpet can stay, but we'll put down plastic I had Thea collect for me today. Once we begin, everyone except Grace and Luke will need to leave the house. Javed has made arrangements for you all to stay at a hotel. When we're finished, we'll call you all back, but the coven and I need total privacy for the ritual."

Heads nodded as items were laid out according to Celina's instructions.

"I've the coven waiting at the top of the driveway, Celina," Thea called.

"Have them come down, then we need them to cleanse before entering the room. I'll go out in a moment with you, Thea, once I'm sure everyone else is gone. Luke, we're going to need you to cleanse too. Thea, can you explain to him what we require?"

clearly terrified, but holding onto hope. The witches entered the room chanting, and the atmosphere deepened.

Celina removed Grace's amulet. "Sisters of the moon, find the points of power," she called.

The women dropped burning sage outside the runes, onto the fireproof floor coverings before moving to points in the room.

Celina raised her gaze to the ceiling, calling, "We beseech thee, mother of power, to give us vision. To let us see the strands which bind this innocent."

The women chanted some more, and Luke's leg bounced as he waited and watched. The women moved, like fish in the sea, seeming to know exactly where they needed to be before completing tasks. Some were blowing on items while others lit more candles.

"Mother of power, we beseech thee to give us the strength to cut these ties that bind this innocent."

The chanting rose in fervour, and a glow rose in the air—large strings of glow. They were intertwined and rising from Grace.

"Mother of power, we beseech thee, grant me the power to remove the veil so she may see."

The colours shone now, a mass of bright greens, reds, and yellows strands which shone as bright as fluorescent lights in the darkness,

"Mother of power, grant thy daughter power," chanted the other women.

Celina scooped up a knife. "Mother of darkness, let this innocent sleep so we may save her past, present, and future. Let us remove the impediments that bind her. Let us bring her peace and serenity."

GRACE LAY on the table so the women could begin. They had explained that it was the best way for them to work on the tether points, and she waited as the women began chanting. She chanced a

look at Luke, the worry on his face locking with the terror that filled Grace.

Would this work? Could she be free?

Whoever this Marrer was, though, Grace knew there was no future until, however she was connected to the demon, she gained her life back.

She stared up at the ceiling, listening to the women chanting.

Then Celina entreated, "Mother of darkness, let this innocent sleep so we may save her past, present, and future. Let us remove the impediments that bind her. Let us bring her peace and serenity," and darkness descended.

It wasn't a true darkness, more that the truth was obscured by an overlay, allowing Grace to hear and feel, but not move or participate. It was a state of limbo, yet she wasn't alone. Sensing another, she reached out with her mind.

"Child, it is time to remove your bindings," a voice said from inside her mind.

"Why?"

Laughter, cool and kind, echoed. "You don't wish to be freed?"

Grace had the sensation of someone watching her. "I do, but I want to live my life free of Marrer. I have a mate. I want…"

"You have many who worry about you. Many who've risked life and limb. You had no such protections before. When you were a child, I did what I could to protect you, but now it is time to relinquish these bindings."

"Who are you?" Grace asked, before the woman, whoever she was, released her.

"I am the mother, the one who knows all. I am the earth and the sky. I am the rain and the sun. I am all."

That doesn't explain anything. *The laughter tinkled again.*

"True, I don't explain, but one day soon, all will be known. Then I shall take my place in my pantheon. But for now, know that I walk beside you, before you, and behind you. You shall be blessed among many and so too your mate. You will be productive and happy, and the darker side of

your soul will be lightened. One day you and your mate shall lead others—not of this world, but another—to a great victory."

What?

"It will come to pass, one day. But for today, it is time for you to return to your own time and place. You will be healed, both in heart and head, when you awaken, so you may overcome Marrer and her evil."

Darkness descended.

LUKE'S ANXIETY rose once Grace closed her eyes. It didn't matter that these women assured him she'd be safe. They were dealing with magic, deep and powerful, and one wrong move or request might end everything.

With each word, Celina moved around the room, scanning the threads, her hands waving aside the knots.

Thea stepped up beside him. "Each knot is a danger point. Cut the thread wrong and the knot moves up, sliding into another strand. Each time the strands touch an unrelated thread, we cause damage, Luke."

He watched, holding his breath as Celina sliced the first thread. It disintegrated and fell away, and he exhaled before tensing as she moved to the next. Over and over, she repeated the process, but as each was sliced it was like more appeared. The strands attached to Grace at neck, legs, head, and body. "It's no wonder she fainted every time," he muttered.

"Shh," Thea hissed.

Partway through someone handed Celina a glass, and she took a quick sip before passing it back, ready to begin once again, it seemed to him.

"Mother of power, we thank thee for thy power, but we beseech you grant us more," Thea murmured, and Celina sent her a thankful smile.

It felt like forever as the women chanted, and Celina prayed and cut at the numerous strings, until there was an obvious change, the threads' glow dimming. Celina hacked and sliced until only one glowing strand remained. The one leading from Grace's heart.

Luke squinted as Celina inspected the string, then turned to him, beckoning.

Stepping off the stool, the stiffness of his body reminded him he'd waited for hours. She reached toward him with the knife.

"Blessed mother, we beseech thee, allow our brother Luke, the mate of our sister, to cut the final thread. May his love and passion heal our sister and give her the freedom of her life."

He stretched out his hand and she placed the knife, frigid and heavy, in his palm.

Closing his hand around the hilt, he moved closer to Grace, who was stretched out on the table.

He reached up and felt the magic exuding. His hand shook, and he bolstered it with the other one, deciding where best to make the cut. He slid the athame to a point and pushed.

Pressure built, then shoved at him, throwing him back against the wall, the knife clattering to the floor, spinning wildly.

Cries of distress and pain filled the room, but he could barely see, liquid obstructing his view. Luke swiped at it and pushed from the floor toward Grace.

Her eyes were open, staring upward. She inhaled deeply then turned, her gaze capturing his. "It is done," she whispered.

Then Grace closed her eyes again.

THIS TIME, Grace rose through the layers of sleep, a sense of well-being and rightness filling her. She opened her eyes to see Luke's face, so beloved, above her.

"Luke," she breathed.

He kissed her, softly but full of emotion. Terror, love, and thankfulness threaded through her in even turns.

"What's wrong?" she whispered when he eventually pulled away.

"You've slept an entire day and into the next night, Grace. Nothing could wake you." His voice was shaky, and his hand sliding over her cheek wasn't stable.

"I'm awake now," she answered, and he sighed.

"True. You need something to eat," he told her, but she shook her head.

"First the bathroom, then I want out of here. Marrer will be building her army, ready to retrieve me."

He rocked back. "You remember?"

Grace nodded. "I do. I know why she needs me, and we need help. But first, let me up." She scooted off the bed and hurried to the bathroom before returning moments later to find him waiting for her. "Okay, food and drink, then we need to talk to... Hang on! What time is it?"

"Closing in on midnight," Luke answered.

She glanced down. "I need jeans and boots and a shirt. Help me dress, then we need the others around, Javed and Celina, Padraic and Fenella. We also need to call on Ba'al Berith and... my father."

It felt weird to suddenly know, after so long, who he was.

"Your father?" Luke queried.

"Vinta. He's a lesser demon but works in Berith's library. He has access to tomes of power. We need that help now."

She stripped off the gown she'd slid on before the ritual, and waited as Luke handed her fresh underwear. Under normal circumstances, she'd have taken a moment to shower, but tonight, that was a luxury she just couldn't afford.

Once dressed, she followed Luke from the bedroom and to the kitchen, where his mother hovered. When she saw Grace, she cried, "Oh, my dear Grace," wrapping her arms around Grace. "You're finally awake! Luke has growled and prowled the day away, worried about you, as have we all."

"Oh!" Grace blinked. "Thank you. But we must hurry, before

daybreak. Luke, can you get everyone to assemble where your house was? We need help and fast. I can feel Marrer's power, and it's growing."

When she saw him staring, Grace laughed. "I'm part demon, remember? I can feel these things. My father may be a librarian, but his mother was of a higher class of Lucifer's personal court. From her I learned to read emotions. Chiefly among them wrath. It slides along the breeze, like a hint of sulphur." She shrugged. "I forgot how much I learned in my two hundred years."

Luke's mouth fell open. "Two hundred?"

"Ah, yes. I guess that makes me older than you." She wanted to snicker, but fear restricted her throat. Did he read it? Could he understand her fears?

"Well, I guess older women do it for me," he muttered. "But later, we're going to talk about a few things."

Fear knotted her guts. "Like?"

"Nothing bad, but clearly the growth of our children isn't going to be quite what I expected."

"Oh." She smiled. "Maybe not, but if we've shared life essence, then you should benefit from that too."

His mother stared at both of them. "Unnatural. You're both so unnatural," she said and stalked away.

"What did...? Did we offend her?"

Luke laughed. "Nah, I think she expected some kind of display of grand passion. But unless you have something in mind, I'm thinking later." He waggled his eyebrows.

Grace giggled. "Yeah, something like that. Now, you make those calls. I've got another task to complete."

"Like?"

"Calling my father and Ba'al Berith. We'll need them both here."

TWENTY-NINE

Grace heard the vehicle before it arrived. *Yet another gift of werehood.* It wasn't a car she knew, but if they were travelling in rentals...well, that made sense, right?

The sweep of lights came closer as both Luke and Grace waited by the ruins of his house. "At least the wards are holding," she muttered, glancing at Thea who waited nearby. "The coven has already drawn the circle, so once we get the plan finalised, we can start to call the demons forth."

"You're sure this will work?" Luke asked.

She shrugged. "Vinta said the ritual should pull Marrer to the location we desire, and allow us to bind her, but if what Berith told us is accurate, she's got a large army. But she doesn't know what I do."

Indeed, the meeting from the night before was etched in her brain.

The group had gathered at the back of Luke's mother's property. Vampires, witches and demons, leprechauns and weres. Anyone looking on would have thought it strange, she thought. But not her. She knew what she was and who. Memories suppressed by a witch were finally uncovered.

"The ritual worked as it should," Celina murmured. "I didn't have a lot of time to finesse it."

"I remember everything. Thank you, Celina. Including the reason Marrer is chasing me. I saw things that she'd rather no one knew. I saw the book she stole, the one with the words to control the demons. What she doesn't know is a page was torn out before she took it. Vinta had impressed on me the power of those books. He'd always said there was no fail-safe if the books fell into the wrong hands. And so, when I had a chance, I regained it."

"For a demon, he certainly has morals," Padraic muttered.

"I heard that, Padraic," Ba'al Berith growled, crowding closer, and Grace might have felt intimidated if it hadn't been for the fact that he wore an air of soberness about him. "We have to shut this down, because while there is a place for chaos in the world, if there is no balance, then all will be lost."

Vinta edged closer. "Sire... my daughter..."

Grace turned to the smaller demonic being present. It had been so long since she'd last seen him. "Hello, Father," she said, then passed him the page. He glanced from her, to it, and back again.

The demon before her stared. "You? My... child? My... Gello?"

"Grace. I'm known as Grace now. And yes, Father." She reached out a hand, turning it so her palm lay upward, just as she always had done as a child. The small act was important to prove her identity, just as much as the words she needed to say. "The library smells of must and old leather, it was the scent of my childhood."

The demon, an imp, blinked, his red eyes glowing in the night, then bowed low to Berith and Luke, his hands shaking while his body shuddered. "You give me... child back. I owe... debt... immense depth," he spoke slowly, as if trying to explain without more words the depths of his gratitude.

Berith lurched forward, now taking on the form of a trim man with dark hair and pale eyes, dressed in jeans and a shirt, just like the others gathered there. "You owe me nothing, Vinta." He spoke gravely, eyes downcast in the moment. "When my child was lost, and when Balala passed over, you were there. You ensured my library remained in order, my days were filled, and my belly too, when it was difficult to know what to do next. When Marrer moved against me, you stood beside me. You are my friend."

Vinta bowed low. "Thank you ...Master." He spoke haltingly, but the meaning was clear.

"We need to summon her," Grace said, and Berith nodded. "Nothing less than that and binding will allow us the time to find out how to defeat her."

"Yes," Berith agreed. "But we need to retrieve the book," he added.

Grace shook her head. "No, because the page I removed? It's the one that will forever change the course of the battle to come."

"You never explained why you lived with your father." Luke stared at her.

"You want to know that now?" Grace frowned. "Alright, short version is my mother was human. She died a long time ago. I don't even remember her. Humans live such short lives, and demons..." She shrugged. "When I was found I was nearly two hundred and fifty years old. I looked around ten because the first years of a demon's life are long, then we mature through adolescence more or less at human rate, because that's when we're vulnerable psychically." She inhaled, oxygen filling her lungs. "Demonic physiology and biology are strange for anyone except ourselves to understand."

Berith stalked over. "We have read the page, the one you stole from Marrer with the instructions." He handed over a page, the hieroglyphs on it difficult for her to discern after so long.

"Father should be the one to read it aloud. It's been too long, and I might make a mistake. We can't afford that, my lord."

"No, we can't, but Vinta isn't here to explain what we have," Berith explained, rubbing his hand over his face.

Grace felt pity for the greater demon. It was his mate who'd created this mess, and he was the one who needed to sort it out.

Padraic stepped forward. "Berith, Danu demands an audience." His face screwed up. "I tried to explain…"

Berith rolled his eyes. "Bloody Danu. Tell her later, once this is done."

Padraic's eyebrow raised, but he lifted the phone in his hand to his ear. "Danu, he said he'll be in touch later. After we complete…"

Grace watched as he scowled into the night, no doubt listening to the goddess' demands.

"No, I am unable to do so," Padraic said. "Yes, I will tell him." There was a long pause. "Yes, I will." He turned to the night and shoved the phone into his pocket.

"She's never changed," Berith said, a touch of impatience in his voice.

"No, and I doubt she will now," Padraic responded.

Celina waved to the witches to join them. "We need to take our positions. Grace, are you ready?"

Luke took her hand. "We're ready," he said forcefully.

Celina smiled. "Then let the fun begin."

CHAPTER

THIRTY

Luke and Grace stepped into the centre of the circle, the grass chipped away, and the earth uncovered was salted, so there was a visible barrier. That would let the coven of witches contain the demon while Celina and Berith bound her. It wouldn't hold her forever, but for now, they sought time.

Luke and Grace stood within a smaller circle in the centre. Their task was to summon Marrer from the depths she'd claimed as her kingdom.

"Once we begin to call her, we cannot leave the circle," Grace reiterated for what felt like the fiftieth time.

Luke knew she was terrified that they might be hurt or taken captive, so he nodded, unruffled by her insistence on reminding him. "I understand that. You said she can't reach us?"

"Not if we stay inside. Once the ritual begins, she'll try to fight the binding, and the witches will keep filling the power of the circle." Grace frowned. "Berith has the page, and Vinta is decoding it now, but it's complicated. I dimly remember the size of her army, but I don't have the power to unmake it. All I can do is show her that I have the page, the one she used to hold onto many of the minions.

But she's held them a long time. All I can be assured of is that she can't increase the size through magic. It's why she wanted me. I think she realised I'd hidden it, so one of Father's friends hid me."

Luke still didn't quite understand the complexities of the situation, but politics had never been his thing; that's why Nate was alpha and not him. "And we can't simply strip her of the power?"

She shook her head. "We need more than we have here. It may even necessitate those with the power going to Ireland to face her on the ground where she's strongest. The land holds power, stronger than we'll have here."

"Huh," he answered. "So we should get started I guess?" He looked across at Celina, who watched them, and he nodded.

In response, Celina raised her hand, and Grace began the demand, "Marrer, we summon you in the name of Lucifer and Ba'al Berith. We invoke the names of all the demons," she said, and she began listing them. "We demand your presence now."

Luke joined in the calls, his hand firmly holding onto Grace, sharing his own latent power to tug the demon onto their presence.

The world around them wavered, but Grace had warned him about that. Marrer would attempt to drag them to her, so he closed his eyes, focusing on repeating after Grace.

"Who dares to summon me?" The voice boomed through the night.

Luke opened his eyes to see the nightmarish creature before him. Ghoulish in the moonlight, she stood nearly seven feet tall, her skin leathery and dark grey, eyes that were slits of obsidian, and her legs and arms tipped with elongated, onyx-coloured nails.

"I, Marrer, Queen of the Underworld, do not simply reply to your command!"

"Marrer, I won't say it's nice to see you again," murmured Grace. "You may not remember me, but I am Gello, daughter of Vinta, under-librarian of the underworld, vassal of Ba'al Berith."

"Gello? Huh, she's dead." The demon's voice echoed through the night.

Grace sighed. "I am part demon and part human, yet my summons has brought you forth."

"For what reason?" Marrer hissed. She stopped her advance, cocked her head so she could look down and see the small circle surrounding Grace and Luke.

"I have the missing page. The one you want above all." Grace lifted it so Marrer could see. It wasn't the real one, but a page they'd worked to ensure it looked like a reasonable facsimile.

The demon roared and made to step in their direction. Luke smiled, ready to play his part. "For a demon, you're sure not the brightest tool in the shed, now, are you? I mean, a child, the daughter of an imp, outwitted you."

"Puny human!" She snarled.

"No human here," he muttered and raised a hand, allowing it to transform just enough that she'd see.

"Were, just what I need in my army," Marrer sneered. "You could do my bidding."

"I don't do anyone's bidding," he answered with a grin. "Except maybe Gello's." They'd all agreed using Grace's previous name was the best option, during the quick planning session where they'd formulated the plan. After all, which demon would look for a Grace? The name wasn't exactly common for demons, or even half ones.

"You dare to correct me?" Her face twisted.

"Now, now, now," he soothed. "When you have a mate... Oh, sorry, you lost yours, didn't you?" He tapped the side of his nose with his paw-shaped hand. "Shame really. Did you look in the lost and found?" Then he laughed. "Ah, never gets old."

They needed to goad her so she'd lose her temper and step into the larger circle which they'd prepared with black lava-infused salt. It had taken more than usual, because Celina had explained the properties in the salt were hampered by the lava impurities. But it was better than dying it.

"Not too much," muttered Grace.

Luke nodded, wiping his hands over his eyes, as if to swipe away tears of laughter.

Marrer took a final step, and Luke felt the echoes through his feet as the circle activated.

Marrer turned. "What? What have you done?" she shrieked, and Celina stepped forward, as did the rest of Thea's coven.

"Blessed mother, we beseech you to bind this demon!" Thea cried, the sound so loud Luke wanted to cover his ears.

Grace's hand twitched in his grasp as the witches began their demands.

Berith now stepped forward as Marrer struggled against the magical, yet barely visible, ropes looped around her body. "I will destroy you," she screeched.

"Marrer, mate of Berith, I deny you the right to arms. I, Berith, librarian of the underworld, bind you to the lesser regions. I, Berith, vassal of Lucifer, destroy your ties to Zazrael and forbid you passage to the upper world."

"You can't do this! I will prevail. I will bring chaos to this world," she cried, her voice sounding dimmer and more remote.

"I, Gello, daughter of Vinta and mate of Luke, vassal of Lucifer, demand that the demon Marrer be bound to the underworld. I beseech my lord and master to make it so," Grace added her voice to the cacophony.

"I, Luke, mate of Gello, daughter of Vinta, and vassal of Nate, add my voice to the binding."

One by one, those present added their demands until finally, a brilliant light flashed and smoke filled the air, sulphurous and cloying. A cough rose in Luke's chest before it cleared, and they stood in the clearing, looking at the spot where Marrer had been moments before.

Luke turned to Grace and asked, "Did we do it?"

She was pale in the moonlight, wavering. "I... Yeah." Then she slumped to the ground.

~

"This is getting a little old," Grace growled as she lay in Luke's arms. Celina and Thea kneeled before her.

"You've expended a lot of magical energy lately," Celina explained. "It stands to reason you're depleted. I'm no doctor, but magic is a demanding master or mistress. You need to take time to recover before we do anything else. My prescription is the two of you take off for a couple of weeks before we reconvene. Go somewhere relaxing. Get on a plane and fly somewhere no one knows you."

Luke grunted. "What about the rest of the demons?"

Grace closed her eyes, trying to work out if there was a possibility they would try to hunt them down.

"Go to Ireland," Berith growled. "We'll need you there soon anyway. We're going to need to bring this to an end."

He stepped back just as a woman appeared in the glade. "Well now, I'm sick of waiting around," she said. "Berith, I sent a message with Padraic—"

"Damn you, Danu. Couldn't you have waited until—" Berith growled.

"Don't you raise your voice at me, you ignorant demon! I said there was something important, and I meant it! Padraic of the Leprechauns, where are you?" She whirled and Grace gaped at the woman, the white dress flaring out while the halter top barely contained her breasts. It would have been very Marilyn Monroe except her hair was flame-red, her face screwed up with anger, and her voice heavily accented, betraying her Irish nationality.

Padraic loped forward. "I did try to tell you, Danu!" he answered, inhaling deeply while Fenella grinned behind him.

"We bound Marrer, Danu. Before she could call up her army of demons," Berith explained, shoving his hands deep into his pockets.

"Oh," Danu answered, and she appeared to slump into herself. "Well, then I guess you don't need me after all."

"Nonsense," Berith protested. "I need you all the more."

Something passed between demon and goddess, but it was fleeting, and Grace didn't consider it again, wondering if she'd imagined it.

"Urgh! You know where to find me," Danu growled and disappeared.

Berith stared where she'd been, and Grace watched Berith until he shook his head and shrugged. "I need to go. The demons who've been released tonight will need me. Vinta, you can stay if..."

The imp slid up beside him. "Return to library. See Gello soon."

Grace pushed herself up and hurried to Vinta before he could disappear. "Wait! Father, I've missed you."

The imp placed his misshapen hand on her shoulder. "Daughter. Mine." Then he smiled, nodded, and was gone.

EPILOGUE

Epilogue

Luke settled into the chair beside Grace, taking her hand. "Well, that's Paula married. Our wedding should be next, or do you want to take off for Ireland first, like Berith suggested?"

Grace snuggled up close to him. "According to Paula, weddings take time to arrange, so I think Ireland, get that out of the way, then we can decide on ours. Besides, I think some time alone is what we need most."

"True. Besides, rebuilding the house will take months." Luke glanced at the people who'd come together to celebrate his sister's wedding. "Mum said she'd oversee it. I think she has her eye on the builder. She's been alone for a long time, and she's ready to mingle again."

"Paula said she's not too old for more babies," Grace added.

Luke coughed and spluttered. "I'm not sure I want to even consider that," he muttered.

Grace laughed. "Yeah, Paula said something similar. I also made an appointment to visit Dr Hastings, and she's arranged for some information from Berith on how our mating will affect our lifespan. She thinks we can count on a couple of millennia at least."

Luke stared at her. "What is that supposed to mean?"

"Well, we'll have plenty of time to start and grow our family. Besides, there's a lot of the world I haven't seen. After all, the ocean is one thing, but the land? I've barely seen anywhere in Australia, and Ireland is little more than a blur. I want to travel, Luke."

He considered her words. "I've seen some of the world, been to England and Scotland, Hong Kong was fun, and so was New Zealand, but America is mostly unknown. You want to do that before having a family?"

"Well, I think that makes sense. After all, once we have kids…" She let the words hang in the air.

He grinned, because he'd caught a vision of her in his mind, heavily pregnant with a child in her arms. It brought a glow of satisfaction with it. "Yeah, sounds good to me." He reached over and pulled her to his chest, feeling the connection and warmth where they touched. "I love you, Grace."

"And I love you, Luke. Forever," she vowed.

"Forever and millennia," he responded.

Berith paced, waiting for Danu to arrive. She'd demanded the time, place, and day, so here he was. Once more waiting.

He caught the tingle of her presence and turned.

In her hand was a bottle, an old wine from centuries ago. "I thought you could use this," she muttered. "I found a letter for you." She handed it over, and as their fingers brushed, he felt a flash of heat.

"What is it?"

"Something Balala had me look after." She shrugged. "Look, I don't know what's in it, but I remember the day she came to me. She was only human, after all. Or was, before she became your consort." Derision threaded the words.

He sniffed and glanced at the paper in his hands, broke the seal.

The words rocked him, and he staggered to the seat, slumped down. "How long?" he demanded, shaking the page in his hand.

"At least four hundred years," she said with a moue of distaste.

"Damn them all," he said, dropping the sheet of paper so he could cradle his head in his hands. "You didn't know?" He lifted his head to spear her with a glance.

Danu shook her head, red hair flying in the still afternoon. "Know what?"

Danu was terrible at lying, having very little guile; he knew that from their long association. So he had to believe her assertion.

He thrust the page at her. She read, the pink of her cheeks bleeding away, leaving her frigidly pale. "No, that can't be right." Her green eyes sparkled in the sunlight. "This can't be true."

Berith shrugged. "We'll need to find out, because if it is…"

"This changes everything," she breathed.

MARRER STORMED THROUGH THE CAVERNS, snarling, and screeching her displeasure for all who could hear. "How could they do this to me? She's still alive, the cunning little bitch." The child, Gello, had caused her all kinds of issues.

The missing page from the *Book of Power* was a problem she'd not found a way to overcome, and her bastard mate, Berith, hadn't given up access to the library, so it wasn't like she could see if there was another copy or even if the copy she'd had somehow magically reappeared there. No, his underlings had controlled the repository and access, and even her underlings hadn't found a way.

Then she'd tried to control access to the fae lands, because they'd written the *Book of Power*. That too had been stymied by the rank bastard, Padraic of the Leprechauns.

And now this! Gello reappearing when she'd had others looking. But while they'd known she was still alive, it was only latent power that had been able to get near her, until that fucking were had found her. *Mated* with her. Now, she was bound to the underworld thanks to Berith and his band of supernatural freaks.

Her last avenue was via Danu, and she doubted that bitch would be a viable avenue to overcome them all. If only Lucifer had granted her the power of Berith when she'd demanded it.

She didn't want to remember the way he'd scoffed at her. That was too much.

"Mistress," an imp implored. "You must read this," he said and tried to shove a tome at her.

She pushed him away. "Be gone! I don't have time for you. I have plans to make, power to take." She whirled, looking at the walls, but even they were closing in on her.

"Mistress!" the creature cried again, and she reached out, catching the imp in her grasp, nails digging deep.

Red mist descended over her vision. "I told you, begone!" The words were guttural and infuriated. She flung the underling to the wall, hearing its gasps and cries. Unholy rage filled her, and she released the power, slamming it into the creature slumped on the floor. "You didn't listen, now pay the price!" Her razor-like fingernails slit its throat. Blood spurted and spattered the walls as the book fell to the floor with a thud.

She returned to her pacing again, the dead imp forgotten on the ground. Once more she began considering what she knew and formulating plans.

"When I get out of here," she muttered.

When...

The End

For Now...

THE BLOOD BRIDE BY IMOGENE NIX

Hope just wants to be an ordinary nestling. She went to college and escaped, but now she's back and there's a secret everyone is keeping from her.

Xavier is the new master of the nest, ready to welcome home the daughter of the house who he has never met. He's unprepared for the woman who steals his breath and enchants him.

Now Hope and Xavier must fight for lives and those of the innocents. After all, it is only by overcoming the rogues that they will have a chance of a timeless future together. But will it be in time?

~

PROLOGUE

As silence descended on the house, the shadows grew—dark grays and blacks that bled into each other. First one figure then another broke away, making a run toward the house. Silent as the grave, they moved swiftly over dew-slicked grass. Then they stopped still. Waiting. Not a movement betrayed them until a signal propelled them back into action and they started crawling upwards. The walls damp coating no barrier to the intruders that ascended in the darkness.

The sound of each window breaking shattered the quiet—the figures were inside. Screams echoed through the night. Yet, in this area of large estates, heavy with noise-absorbing shrubbery, no one could hear those within. The blood-curdling screams went on and on before finally dying away.

Just one sound echoed through the night: The sobbing of a child.

The front door opened and figures trooped out—ghostly specters against an inky night sky, broken by a single outline. A child in white, carried at the center of the pack.

No sound broke the silence as they moved toward the trees surrounded the house.

Flames now licked at the manor: A deathly glow of oily smoke rising.

All that remained was a single person—wrapped in a cape of midnight blue beyond the house—watching them melt away.

Jemima moved toward the burning structure, breaking into a run as she breached the threshold. Vainly she attempted to enter, but the heat drove her back.

Now dashing tears from her face, she raced across the graveled driveway toward the gates, where the guardhouse was located. No sign of life existed within the building and some instinct of survival slowed her pace to a careful creep. Out of breath and heaving from exertion, she nervously checked within.

Small puffs of white vapor colored the glass. She darted from one window to another. Her cloak drawn tightly around her body, hoping it would camouflage her from sight.

Satisfied, Jemima entered through the heavy, wooden front door and moved toward the phone she spied on the floor. Her eyes darting here and there she dialed, listening to the rotary motor as it returned to the proper position. Time was short and if *they* came back, she needed to have shared the message.

The phone rang once. Twice. With a brrping sound it connected.

"Hello?" A male answered and she felt a warm flush of relief at the voice. A voice she knew well.

"The manor has been breached. The girl child taken." The words erupted and her hand trembled.

"On our way." The click of the receiver being replaced echoed loudly in the stillness of the room.

Copper. She smelled copper.

Her stomach soured, knowing it meant more deaths. Jemima looked around for the gun—a gun with deadly, holy water-infused copper bullets—she knew was hidden somewhere in the room. A gun she couldn't find. *No divine intervention exists here*, she thought.

Hopefully *they* didn't remain. Feeding. If they were still here, that's what they would be doing. She found a corner and scrunched down, hiding from sight.

Crouched low, she tried to stay as still as possible, listening for sounds of the vehicles she knew would be coming. She dug her fingers into the flesh of her arms; remaining aware enough to stop before drawing blood. That would surely bring them out. Jemima dragged the cloak around her to capture the warmth, yet there was little to be found.

The sounds of engines roused her from the corner of the room.

Jemima inched toward the window, the lead of the old glass distorting her view, hearing raised voices she knew Mistress Cressida had arrived.

Jemima retreated. Remained hidden from the woman because if she knew, all may well be lost. From the shadowed room she listened to the conversation…

"It smells like Estersham." The Mistress' eyes closed. "If it is, we have a problem." She turned once more, her face set and eyes now glacial in intensity. "James?"

The man nodded as if he knew what was to come.

"If I take those steps, I cannot return. Another must stand in my place." Her voice hardened while her eyes glittered in the dim light, piercing in their intensity.

Then the Mistress' voice called out in the near silence. "You and yours have been my loyal servants for so many years. I took an oath to protect you long ago. I renewed it with marriage and births, over and over. Now, my home and yours have been breached and this child taken from us. The girl child, who will be the hope and salvation of our kind, was ripped from the bosom of our nest. I will repay your loyalty and I will get her back." The words of power rippled in the night and licked at Jemima's skin.

Available in Ebook
books2read.com/BloodBride-Nix

Direct Autographed Copy
https://www.imogenenix.net/BloodBride

THE RESET

A zombie apocalypse is here, but figuring out how to survive in the immediate aftermath is only the first step.

Elaine is just an ordinary woman, but when the apocalypse occurs, she must find a way to survive in an increasingly hostile world. Enter Liam, the policeman who saves her at their first meeting and provides assistance as they try to cope with the zombie outbreak brought about by an unknown infection that's spreading out of control.

Together they form a community, trying to save as many lives as they can, a place where people can be safe. Even in the throes of disaster though, emotions creep up, taking both of them by surprise. Who knows? They might just get their happy ever after...if they can survive.

Elaine's fingers curled over the radio, her heart stuttering with fright.

"Officials are unable to determine the cause of the illness breaking out all over the city, but urge calm. If you are cornered by the infected, seek safety. Should you be bitten, seek medical attention immediately."

Her fingers fluttered against her lips. The dirge rose, long moans as those infected, their skin turning a deep grayish green and their eyes milky white, howled outside the office. Elaine pushed the curtain aside once more and glanced through the glass. The collection had grown, their faces slack yet eerily aware that she remained inside.

"I don't know what to do." She turned back to watch as her boss, William Eckerman, rocked in his seat. "I mean, we've been holed up here for over two days. There's no food in the kitchenette, the toilet is overflowing, and we can't stay here, otherwise we'll die." The jitter of her stomach warned her that panic was rising up, about to overwhelm her.

"Elaine, relax. It's just a precautionary measure. The police will come and..."

"The police have indicated that they are overwhelmed. Military forces are on the way, but communications are hampered by the...by the walking dead converging on sites with power. In the latest update, the government is ceasing all non-urgent tasks. They're recommending that you hunker down and hope you can ride it out. Resources are limited, and it's suggested that, if possible, you should stock up and find a safe location in which to secure yourself." The announcer's voice shook.

"See? They're saying we need to find a secure location, stock up, and hide. Mr. Eckerman, we can't stay here." The urge to flee coursed through her veins like an exploding freight train. "We have to go to our homes. Be with our families."

He flicked invisible specks of lint from his immaculate sleeves and rocked again in the seat. "Well, Elaine, I think, given your current level of excitation, you should certainly go home."

She frowned at the cool tone. "Uhhh, Mr. Eckerman?" "Yes?"

"Mr. Eckerman—"

"When this is over, I'll give you an excellent reference for the four years of service. It's sad that something has overset you to the point where completing your work is no longer your priority. I understand it is probably time to expand your employment horizon."

As she stood there listening to the drivel he was spouting, growing anger warred with her terror. "Mr. Eckerman..."

"Go on and get your things together. It's best you go directly home."

She shuffled to her desk, shock assaulting her as she gathered the few personal items she'd stashed. The photo of her parents, the Mickey Mouse cup she'd bought at a major attraction. The hairbrush and small clutch of cosmetics joined the rest of her belongings, then Elaine straightened, turned, and headed for the door.

"Aren't you forgetting something?" Mr. Eckerman held out his hand, and she blinked. "Umm, what?"

"Keys."

She blinked again then made an 'O' with her mouth. "I forgot them when I came in. I'll have to drop them off once everything is done."

He snarled and opened the door. "Go on then. I want them back here as soon as the situation is cleared."

She looked outside, glad he'd insisted on staff using the back door, which was protected by the security fencing and remote-controlled roller door. She hurried to her vehicle, pleased it was older and heavier, sure it would protect her until she reached home.

Leaving the building was scarier than she expected. As she drove the short distance she constantly glanced around, seeing small huddles here and there of those who were infected. Each time they lurched in her direction she panted, heartrate increasing, adrenaline spiking until she was past them.

Turning onto her street left her amazed. Smoking wrecks of cars littered the street, and several gray-skinned individuals loitered. She drove carefully, hoping she could make it home without being waylaid.

When she reached her house she swung in to park on the road, thinking she'd have plenty of time to get in the house without any of the walkers in the way. She found the key for the front door, checked the rearview mirror to make sure none of the infected were close by, then got out of the car. Slamming the car door shut, she engaged the locks and sprinted to her front door.

Fighting the jamb until the door eased open, Elaine slid within and pushed the door shut. The tiny house on the outskirts of town she shared with her best friend had a deserted feel to it.

"Emily?" Once sure the door was securely latched she hurried up the hall, calling her friend's name. Every door she opened and peered inside was empty, and at the end of ten fruitless minutes she slumped down in a kitchen chair.

Liam wasn't sure what to do. The supermarket was empty, and shelves of food were scattered on the floor as he picked his way along the aisles.

"They said to lay in supplies then hunker down." He glanced at the phone in his hand. "They didn't say to break into the super-market though." Ramon, his half-brother, snickered into the camera of the phone, and Liam shrugged.

They'd flown into Canberra three days ago and settled into the tiny B-and-B on the edge of this township. The location seemed great, only a few miles from Parliament House. It was close to the venue of the three-day conference he was attending on policing in emergency situations. Ramon had come because he'd concluded his last contract in an African country with a bubonic plague epidemic and was at a loose end.

No one could have expected something like this outbreak to occur though, and food was a priority. Liam had insisted Ramon stay at the B-and-B. Having a brother who was an epidemiologist and infection prevention specialist meant he might be called upon by the authorities for assistance, and they couldn't afford for him to be infected by the virus.

"Okay, I'll see what I can find and get back there as quickly as I can." Liam disconnected the call and turned to scan the shelves. "Long-life milk, because it will be good for at least a year on the shelf, sugar, coffee. Bottled water. Some powdered milk as well." He thrust them into the trolley and moved as quickly as he could toward the end of the aisle.

A groan stilled him. He'd already seen the results of those infected, the way they set upon victims, the dripping, bloody teeth. If that moan was anything to go by, he was no longer alone in the shop.

"Get back!" The startled words of a woman almost had him jumping.

"Hello?" He cursed inwardly for now making himself a target as the sound of shambling footsteps echoed, moving in his direction.

"He's heading your way!" the woman yelled as the gray man turned the corner, eyes blank, mouth slack through dripping trails of scarlet. The outstretched hands moved toward him. He didn't have anything on him that would be considered a weapon and cursed that decision. The paperwork for going armed in public—something the department had been cracking down on lately—would have been worth it after all.

The creature extended its arms and gave an "uhhh" sound, and he pondered for a moment whether there was some way to disable it. The thought came and went when the woman screamed and a second and third shuffler made its way in his direction.

The handle of the trolley was just in reach and he tugged it backward, braced his legs, then ran in the direction of the shuffler. The trolley hit the creature in the chest, and it went down, legs and arms waving frantically until it rolled. Now the sound that emanated from its mouth became more of a growl of fury.

He reached out, his hand curling around the nearest can. Saying a silent prayer, he aimed and threw. The crack of heavy metal on bone and the spray of blood as the man went down without a whimper gave him momentary pleasure, but not before the woman from the next aisle scurried around to him.

"There's two more," she screamed.

He didn't glance at her, merely reached up, grabbed another tomato soup can, and lobbed. It hit without the power to cease the onward march.

"Dammit!"

"I've... There's some kitchen string here. Would that help?"

He turned briefly and acknowledged the beautiful, curvy, red-haired woman thrusting the plastic-wrapped item at him, but he shook his head as they stumbled backward.

"We're going to need something a little more useful." He considered what might be here in this tiny store as the woman disappeared before returning with two long, metal-headed rakes. "What about these?" she asked.

He laughed, grabbed one out of her hands as the walkers came within reach, and thwacked it down hard on the head of the nearest one. The rake dropped with a thud and rolled under the shelving unit.

She made a sound, rather like a moan, and turned away as he snatched the other implement and used it to push the other shuffler back.

This time he lined up the male, sidestepped its attempt at grabbing him, then swung this new rake like a bat. The infected individual fell to the floor, and he brought the rake down on its head. She turned and retched while he waited.

"They're... Those were humans! Why did you—"

"No, they aren't humans anymore. They were zombies, and they'll kill you as soon as look at you. Now grab what you need so we can get out of here."

He glanced down one last time at the remains he'd left on the floor. He felt bad about what he'd had to do, but sugarcoating the truth wouldn't make it any better. The only thing they could do was stock up and get back to safety.

He threw tins and jugs into the trolley, along with frozen items, which he was sure would only be available for a little while longer. He also tossed in other essentials such as toilet rolls. He noted that the woman, tears flowing down her cheeks, followed his lead.

Then, with both trolleys full, they left the store and headed to the carpark. This was the danger time. He pulled out his cellphone and dialed Ramon. "Hey, I've got a full load and I'm heading in."

"Good, 'cause I'm hungry and the radio is just repeating what we already know."

He turned to the woman. "Will you be all right to get home?"

She sniffled inelegantly and nodded. "I'm just over the road there." She pointed to the

tiny cottage beside the B-and-B residence where he was staying, and he laughed. When she glanced at him, he sobered. "I'm right next door."

"Oh."

Available from Love Books Publishing
https://books2read.com/Reset

Direct Autographed Copy
https://imogenenix.net/product/the-reset/

A VERY MERRY WIDOW

A Very Merry Widow

Louisa thought she'd made the right choice. Jeremy had been the man she'd loved, but he wasn't who she thought he was. After he dies in a horse riding accident, she wants more. Not another husband, but perhaps a lover who'd fulfilled her needs while she raised her daughters.

Albert never expected to return to England, let alone to take up the family seat or the title of Earl of Conney. Yet here he was, returning from the wilds of Australia, with his friend, Frederick. A convicted felon. He'd sworn to himself if he was going to assume the title, he'd use the influence that went with it to clear his friends name. Brothers-in-law, Langdon Devereaux and Aeddan Fitzsimmons are the connections he needs, and they bring him into the contact with Louisa Lavenwood, a beautiful and aloof widow with two gorgeous but young daughters.

But she has a dark secret, and this unwilling hero feels the need to save her. Along the way passion explodes and they're helplessly lost in its thrall; if only they can overcome the danger, then perhaps more than passion lies in their future.

Louisa watched as the casket containing the body of her husband, Jeremy, was lowered into the ground. His coffin of dark oak and silver fittings shone in the weak daylight, and emotional numbness filled her senses. The fog of the morning had lifted a little, but the cold seeped into her bones as she dragged the heavy, black shawl close around her shaking body. The sounds of weeping from her mother-in-law beside her had been her companion since the accident. Now with the funeral passed, there was only the wake left to survive, then she could consider what came next. Where her future lay.

Her hand, clenched in a black kid glove, was slightly obscured by the black mourning veil she wore as she wiped at her cheek, hoping they'd not look too closely and know. Black would be the only colour she'd wear for a year because convention dictated it, followed by another year of grey, half-mourning. She hated knowing that she would be restricted again.

The bombazine of her gown, heavy and stiff, dragged at her body as her mind whirled with everything and nothing.

Since Jeremy's death, so many emotions had enveloped Louisa, but she'd held them tight within her breast.

Fury that he'd been so stupid as to be riding in a storm.

Grief that the man she'd loved had been taken from her.

But most of all, *betrayal*, because she knew who he'd been with.

There was more, she just knew it, but hadn't yet had time to enquire of her family's man of business. A man like Jeremy, one who'd lied to her face, who'd strayed just days before she gave birth... The truth was coming out, and she welcomed it with a vicious stab of honesty.

A storm was brewing—rage growing—and if *her ladyship* thought she'd simply keep quiet and sweet, she was in for a startling awakening. The roiling fury had grown in the last three days, and she promised herself that soon, she'd release the poison and begin to heal.

As soon as the requirements of widowhood were done, Louisa told herself as her eyes stung.

Exhaustion dragged at her weary mind.

She barely heard the words of the minister, committing her husband's remains to the ground.

All she knew was, with a child and a newborn babe, she was a widow. Alone in a man's world.

A hand reached out, took hers. *Elspeth*. Both her sisters, Isabelle and Elspeth and their husbands had made the trek back to the family home to support her when she needed them most. Men who were well-born. Men who she hoped would protect her from her mother-in-law's vicious tongue. Men who would protect her while she learned what she needed to know and while she decided what her future would look like.

Now wasn't the time to explain. There hadn't been time to do so before the funeral, but once Jeremy's family left, her sisters and brothers-in-law would hear all. It wouldn't be pretty, but she'd need their support. To make plans. Not just for herself but also her daughters.

Dirt was pressed into her hands, and she glanced down at it. "You need to throw it," Elspeth muttered.

She followed the instruction without a word, crouching down to ensure it thudded on the lid of the casket. Then she stayed there for a moment, silently considering. Finally, she rose.

The minister extended his hands. "I'm so very sorry for your loss."

She whispered something. It was probably the right words, but right now, she held tight to her control, the only thing that had bolstered her for the last few days. Ever since learning of Jeremy's betrayal and death.

At the gate, the carriages waited, one for her and her sisters. Their husbands would ride beside the jet-black conveyance. Another waited for Jeremy's grieving parents, and the rest of the family who'd attended had arranged their own transport.

Walking to the vehicle, silence echoed, apart from the cry of a crow. The sound crass and discordant.

Awareness that his family followed was cloying. Freedom was what Louisa craved most right now. Her sisters would surely see that and understand.

It was only once they were settled inside the carriage and it was moving that she took their hands. "Thank you for coming, sisters. We must talk. But after his family leaves." Her voice sounded scratchy from the night before, sobbing into the pillow that still faintly echoed the scent of Jeremy.

"Of course we would come." Isabelle patted her hands.

"You needed us, so we're here," Elspeth offered.

Looking at her sisters, both married with their own children, and returned to England, she wondered if she'd been too young. Too innocent. Too unaware when she'd accepted Jeremy. Thoughts of that day, the gown she'd worn, and the flush of success had gulled her into accepting a flawed man.

Her sisters had been initially concerned but had relented after she'd told them she wanted no one else. They acquiesced and as a young girl of seventeen she'd married Jeremy.

Now at twenty-three, she was a widow in black.

Jeremy's family had finally left as the night drew in. Dinner was quiet in the formal dining room; the staff brought her favourite—a solid and warming meal. The staff, even now, stood with her, protecting her as did her own family. Now, settled around the large fire in the parlour, she would tell them everything.

Isabelle and Elspeth crowded in beside her. Warming her more effectively than the fire could, while their husbands, Aeddan and Langdon, filled the wing chairs. They were strong, reliable men, and the right partners for her sisters, Louisa knew.

"What do you wish to tell us, dearest?" Elspeth gripped her hands.

"He... Jeremy. The night of the accident? He'd been out. There was a tremendous storm which blew in and he ventured home in it. But he'd... He had a mistress, Elspeth. A woman in the neighbouring township. He'd been with her."

Silence descended on the room. "You're sure?" Aeddan leaned forward, imbuing the question with power.

"Yes. I received a note yesterday. Before your arrival." She fished about in the pocket of her gown and drew it out with shaking hands. "Here, read it for yourself."

She didn't wish to ever see it again. The memory imprinted on her mind.

Dear Mrs Lavenwood,
Allow me to offer my condolences. Dearest Jeremy and I were as
close as any man and woman could be. He confided in me, prior to
the accident, that your recent interesting state and the doting on
your daughter were difficult for him. He was a man who needed to

be first in everything, including your affections, especially given his unfortunate position at birth.

However, it is my expectation that a token of his regard will be forthcoming to me. My expenses do not end with Jeremy's death as there is a child. As such, I feel it is only right, in light of the closeness we shared, that I should be granted a portion of his fortune, which I understand he personally used to purchase your family home.

I will, of course, be more than willing to engage with your solicitor at a time that is convenient to him.

Lady Pamela Jezerey

Aeddan swore and thrust the paper to Langdon, whose eyes glittered with fury as he read the missive. The paper then was read by both Elspeth and Isabelle.

"He had no claim on the house?" Aeddan queried. "So, he cannot gain any control of the Forster Shipping money or property?"

Elspeth shook her head. "When we drew up the marriage settlement, both Isabelle and I ensured the house did not pass from the family's control, nor any of the business. Louisa was young, and it was the best way we could protect her. The portion that went to Louisa was significant, but was not used in any way for the upkeep of the house or to pay the staff. They were all in the employ of Forster Shipping."

Langdon smiled. "And of course, he duly signed that?"

"Oh yes," Isabelle said with a smile. "We had our man of business bring in a senior solicitor from London to ensure everything was watertight. We love our sister." She shrugged then turned to Louisa. "We wanted to ensure her needs and those of any children were protected."

Aeddan stood and stalked to the fireplace, looked at it for a long moment. "With regards to this child this woman is claiming is your husband's. Has anyone questioned the veracity of her claim? That the child..."

Langdon nodded. "Yes, I agree. We need to establish if indeed the child was Jeremy's."

"No. I don't wish you to do that. Not openly or behind my back." Too many things had occurred, things Louisa knew nothing about until now, and she'd not allow anyone to hide this kind of information from her. Never again.

"But dearest," Elspeth stated, but stilled as Louisa shook her head.

"But you should know, Louisa. If the child *is* his... His parents should take some kind of steps."

Her laugh was discordant. "No, they won't. If this child is his, it's a bastard..." She huffed, because she knew that sounded callous. "I don't know the right answer, but if I've learned anything during this time, it's that his family shies away from truths that do not conform with their norm. Now then, I need to make decisions. Good decisions."

"But the child..." Isabelle leaned in. "It's innocent. It should be protected."

Louisa shook her head. "If there's a child, and I don't know the answer, what if it's not his?"

"Then we find out," answered Langdon. "Once the truth is known, then you can make a decision."

Louisa bit her lip, hearing for the first time the truth in his words. "Find out then," she whispered. "If it's not..."

"You have no responsibility," answered Isabelle.

"Perhaps now is the time to travel up to our properties," Elspeth added. "Take some time away while this is—"

Louisa inhaled deeply, felt the air in her chest, and prepared herself mentally. "Elspeth, much as I would love to run away from all this, you've both sheltered me for far too long. It's time I stood on my own. Took control of my life. I intend to see this through and to become an equal shareholder in Forster Shipping. I have two daughters who need to see their mama as an independent woman, and for too long, I allowed others to direct my life and felt secure in the lack of knowledge. If I've learned nothing else, it's that I'm strong and capable."

Louisa sat upright in the chair and stared forward at first one then the other sister.

When they both opened their mouths to remonstrate, Louisa held up a hand. "No. It's true. I will no longer be passive, sisters. I will see this mess of Jeremy's through, and as for Jezerey, well, whatever you learn will be dealt with by the solicitors. There is a full year of black, then when I can wear other colours. This is the time when I will consider my options."

This new Louisa was merely the tip as plans and ideas were unveiling in her mind. Not yet fully formed, but beginning to cascade. *I need time.* Time to let go of the dream, time to formulate her plan, and time to unravel the threads of a life barely lived before she could decide what and who the new Louisa would be.

"Living here? It's no longer enough, and I will need your support soon. Lady Constance is most insistent I should move to the Hall..." Before her sisters could speak, Louisa held up a hand. "...which I have no intentions of doing. She plans to take control of me and my life and my daughters' lives too. That I will not tolerate. Just as I will not tolerate her waspish friends and their whispers."

"We'll put paid to the biddies, my love," Elspeth answered. "You'll have our unwavering support and those of our circle. All you need to do is ask."

"Good," she said. "Because I've already sent for our man of business and the solicitor from London. I will stand on my own two feet, and I will protect what is mine and ours."

Available from Love Books Publishing
https://books2read.com/MerryWidow

Direct Autographed Copy
https://imogenenix.net/product/a-very-merry-widow/

Also by Imogene Nix

<u>**Warriors of the Elector**</u>

- Star of Ishtar
- Starline
- Starfire
- Star of the Fleet
- Starburst
- The Star of Eternity

The Star of Ishtar & Starline - Print

Starfire & Star of the Fleet - Print

Starburst & The Star of Eternity - Print

<u>**Blood Secrets**</u>

- The Blood Bride
- The Illuminated Witch
- The Sorcerer's Touch

<u>***The Secrets World:***</u>

<u>**Blood Secrets**</u>

- The Blood Bride
- The Illuminated Witch
- The Sorcerer's Touch

<u>**House Secrets**</u>

- As Dawn Breaks

- Immortal Consequences
- Edge of Night

All That Glitters - a House Secrets Novella

Danu's Secrets

- The Downfall of Padraic O'Shaunessy
- A Demon Called Grace
- The Secrets of Danu

The Automaton Series

- Haven House
- Nobel Crest

The Search Duology

- Miss Elspeth's Desire
- Miss Isabelle's Craving

Duology World Novels

- A Very Merry Widow

Reunion Trilogy

- War's End
- The Assassin
- Executing Justice

The Reunion Trilogy in Paperback

Sex Love & Aliens

- Tangled Webs

- False Webs
- Covert Webs

21st Testing Protocol

- Cyborg: Redux
- Children Of A Greater Evil
- When Evil Came To Stay
- Finis: The War To End All Wars

Celtic Cupid Trilogy

- Blame The Wine
- A Stranger's Embrace
- Revenge On Cupid

The Celtic Cupid Trilogy in Paperback

Zombieology

- The Reset
- I Dream of Zombies
- The Six Million Dollar Zombie
- Make Room For Zombies
- Days of Our Zombies
- Unnamed Zobiology title

Out Of Time Series

- Flight In time (coming in 2025)
- Bound In Time (coming in 2026)
- Running Out of Time (coming in 2026)

Knights of Pleasure

- Silken Knights

<u>Single Titles</u>

The Chocolate Affair (also in Print)

Falling In Love Again (Previously A Sapphire For Karina)

BioCybe (also in Print)

Hesparia's Tears (also in Print)

Tomorrow's Promise (also in Print)

A Bar In Paris (also in Print)

Inheritance Of The Blood (also in Print)

The Plan (also in Print)

Loving Memories (also in Print)

Hero of Heartbreak Hill (also in Print)

My One & Only (also in Print)

Curse Bound (also in Print)

<u>Non Fiction</u>

Self Publishing: Absolute Beginners Guide (With Suzi Love)

<u>Written as Ciara Cave</u>

25 Curated Ways To Get Rid Of Telemarketers

Book Signings for Absolute Beginners

ABOUT THE AUTHOR

 Imogene is published in a range of romance genres including Paranormal, Science Fiction and Contemporary. She is mainly published in the UK and USA.

In 2010, Imogene Nix (the pen name not Imogene herself) was born. Imogene sat down and worked tirelessly for 3 months culminating in the book Starline, which became the first in a trilogy titled, "Warriors of the Elector." Since then she's had over 30 titles published and is now focusing on hybridising herself - with a mixture of traditionally published and self-published works.

In fact, she's taking control of many of her back catalogue books, which are slowly re-releasing as self-published titles.

Imogene is a member of a range of professional organisations world wide, and believes in the mantra of mentoring and paying it forward and is actively involved in mentorship (through NaNoWrimo and her vlog: In The Chair With Imogene Nix) and tutoring of new and upcoming authors.

In her spare time she loves to drink coffee, wine & eat chocolate and is parenting her spoiled dog and a ferocious cat along with her husband and daughter and looks forward to weekends away with her husband in their caravan "The Seven Year Hitch!" Do look forward to her caravan romance at some point!

To Contact Imogene
www.imogenenix.net
imogene@imogenenix.net

Sign up for her newsletter at
https://www.imogenenix.net/Signup

facebook.com/ImogeneNix
x.com/ImogeneNix
instagram.com/ImogeneNix
bookbub.com/authors/imogenenix

www.ingramcontent.com/pod-product-compliance
Lightning Source LLC
Chambersburg PA
CBHW070633170726
48291CB00003B/993